STAY

STAY

The Last Dog
in Antarctica

Jesse
Blackadder

ABC
Books

The ABC 'Wave' device is a trademark of the Australian Broadcasting Corporation and is used under licence by HarperCollins*Publishers* Australia.

First published in Australia in 2013
by HarperCollins*Publishers* Australia Pty Limited
ABN 36 009 913 517
harpercollins.com.au

HarperCollins*Publishers*
Level 13, 201 Elizabeth Street, Sydney NSW 2000, Australia
Unit D1, 63 Apollo Drive, Rosedale, Auckland 0632, New Zealand
A 53, Sector 57, Noida, UP, India
1 London Bridge Street, London, SE1 9GF, United Kingdom
2 Bloor Street East, 20th floor, Toronto, Ontario M4W 1A8, Canada
195 Broadway, New York, NY 10007, USA

National Library of Australia Cataloguing-in-Publication entry:

Blackadder, Jesse.
    Stay : the last dog in Antarctica / Jesse Blackadder.
    ISBN: 978 0 7333 3177 0 (pbk.)
    For ages 9–12.
    Theft—Juvenile fiction.
    Guide dogs—Statues—Tasmania—Hobart—Juvenile fiction.
    Guide dogs—Statues—Antarctica—Juvenile fiction.
A823.4

Cover design by Christa Moffitt, Christabella Designs
Front cover images supplied courtesy of Jesse Blackadder
Back cover image: Stay with penguins by Jenny Feast
Author photograph by Dave Hosken
Typeset in ITC Stone Serif by Kirby Jones

For Aimee

Before you read this book ...

Stay is real. She has been living in Antarctica since 1991.

Some of the adventures in this story are based on Stay's real ones and some are imaginary. No one really knows what Stay has been up to all this time.

The people in this story have all been made up.

This story is set in the early 1990s. Back then, people in Antarctica relied on high-frequency radio for communication. Telexes (printed messages like telegrams) were common. Letters could only be sent and received when ships came — just a few times a season. Sometimes expeditioners could make short, very expensive INMARSAT phone calls back home on a line that crackled and echoed, and which was really only used for emergencies. The buildings they lived and worked in were old and cold. They still used huskies and sledges to travel around, as well as quad bikes, Hägglunds over-snow vehicles and tractors. There were many more men than women working in Antarctica, but the numbers of women were increasing each season.

Stay arrived in Antarctica just as the huskies were being taken out and the new ANARESAT satellite communication systems were being installed at each station. New buildings were being erected — it was the end of an era of isolation.

Nowadays people living in Antarctica have landlines, email and internet access. The buildings are more modern and comfortable. People working out in the field carry personal GPS units to track their way safely back. Women are present in all the professions working in Antarctica.

But lots of things about living in Antarctica haven't changed. It is still a big adventure and can still be dangerous! The food is just as great and, because of the cold, you can eat things that are years past their use-by date.

You can read more about Stay's real Antarctic life at the end of this book.

Chapter 1

The woman raised her hand. 'Stay, Girl,' she said. Then she laughed and patted the dog on the head. 'I guess you don't have much choice, eh?'

Girl felt the weight of the hand on her head, but she didn't move. Like all Labradors, she tried to be obedient.

Jet, the black Labrador, wagged his tail. *You'll be OK, Girl*, he wuffed. *Don't forget what I told you.* He pulled a little at his handle to get the woman's attention.

Carol looked down at him. 'Time to go home, is it, Jet?' She crouched and snapped the padlock shut on the chain around Girl's leg, then gave her one last pat as she stood up. 'Bye-bye, Girl. Your new paint job looks wonderful — I'm sure you'll do an even better job for us now.'

Girl watched them walking away down the street. Jet padded close to Carol's legs, guiding her through the throng of people. He stopped at the kerb when Carol wanted to cross the road and waited obediently till she said, 'Forward,' and they stepped off the pavement together. Girl lost sight of them on the other side of the road.

She sighed. She wished she could follow Jet back to Carol's nice warm house and sit in front of the fireplace, but she couldn't. Although she was a golden Labrador, she wasn't a flesh-and-bone dog: she was made of fibreglass. Her job was to sit still in one place and remind people how important Guide Dogs were. She had a coin slot in her head — rather undignified, she thought — and she would look up with her big brown painted eyes and try to will people to put money into it. The funds she raised would help train new Guide Dogs.

It was spring, but the day felt icy. Hobart, Australia's southernmost city, was on the banks of the Derwent River, which flowed down to the Southern Ocean. After that there was nothing but water all the way to Antarctica. Girl knew all about Antarctica. Before she'd been sent back to the factory for repainting, she'd spent months sitting outside an electronics shop. The televisions in the window were on all night long, and Girl watched them when it got lonely. She'd learnt a lot about humans, but her very favourite program had been about Antarctica.

The workday was ending. The shopping strip closed with a clatter of roll-down doors. A cold wind whistled along the street and people hurried past with their heads down. No one looked at Girl. They all wanted to get home. A few drops of rain started to spit.

The street emptied until Girl was all alone. The shop window behind her was lit by a neon sign and she was bathed in blue light. There weren't any televisions nearby for Girl to watch. She would have shivered if she could. By now, Jet would be curled up by the fire with Carol. He was nearly ready to be paired with a blind person and start working as a Guide Dog. He'd have a real owner and a real home of his own. His job was to go everywhere with his owner and keep him or her safe. He didn't have to stay on the cold street outside a supermarket like Girl did, without even a television to watch.

A seagull flapped down and landed at Girl's paws. A few chip crumbs were crushed on the footpath and the bird waddled around pecking them up, making little squawking noises. Girl watched her. Even a seagull didn't have to stay in one spot, but could fly anywhere.

Imagine if she could fly ...

Girl pictured herself opening her wings, taking a few steps and flapping into the sky just like the seagull. She'd swoop over the rooftops and across the park to the big trees. From there she could fly to the docks, where the big ocean-going ships were moored.

Squark! The gull shrieked in surprise and took off. *Clunk!* A coin was shoved through the slot in Girl's head and clattered down into her empty insides, and a big hand patted her.

'Good girl!' a man's voice said as he walked off, his footsteps echoing along the street.

When she'd recovered from the surprise, Girl reminded herself to keep a sharper lookout for humans coming with money. She sniffed the air. She could smell salt water and fish drifting up faintly from the Hobart docks in the direction the gull had flown.

If only she could have adventures! She'd been told to 'stay' by Carol, and she always did what she was told, but she wished with every fibre of her fibreglass being that she could be a real dog like Jet and go on her own adventures.

Girl had only met Jet the day before, but even in that short time she'd learnt a lot about real dogs. She could understand when Jet spoke and he could read her thoughts perfectly. Before long they were talking like old friends.

Jet hadn't thought her dreams were silly. He'd listened, with his head cocked to one side and his pink tongue hanging out, and given a little whine. 'Maybe you will have adventures. You never know, Girl.'

It got dark and a little more rain fell. Girl wondered how long she'd have to stay outside the supermarket. Would Carol come back for her tomorrow? Or perhaps the day after?

Way off up the street she heard voices. She pricked up her ears. Who was coming? Whoever they were, they were singing and their voices were horribly out of tune. She could hear footsteps — five sets of them — and by the sound of it they were unsteady.

As they came closer, she tried to make herself invisible, but it didn't work.

'Look at that!' one of them cried, stopping in front of her. 'A dog!'

His friends laughed. 'That's the sort of dog they want us to have,' another said. 'Plastic.'

I'm not plastic, I'm fibreglass, Girl thought firmly.

The man dropped to his knees. 'Ouch,' he said. He grabbed hold of Girl to steady himself. 'Good dog. Aren't you a good girl?'

The others laughed. 'Come on, Chills. Leave the poor dog alone.'

'No dogs!' He looked sadly into Girl's eyes. 'You know that? They won't let us have dogs any more.'

'You'll have to take a toy dog,' another one of them said. 'Now come *on*, Chills! It's late. We've got to board at dawn.'

The man called Chills looked at her for a few more moments. His eyes were bright and she wondered if he was going to cry.

Girl remembered what Jet had told her. *I'm lonely*, she thought in Chills's direction. *And I dream of adventures.*

He leant forwards and gave her a hug, and his arms were warm and friendly. It was the first time anyone had ever hugged her. When his friends pulled him to his feet and led him away, Girl thought she might cry too. It was even lonelier and darker after they had disappeared. Feeling very sorry for herself, Girl started to doze.

She woke with a start a few hours later. Something was over her head, blinding her. She couldn't see a thing. She heard a sharp crunch and the chain fell from her leg with a metallic clatter. She could feel herself being lifted up and carried. She was being dognapped! She wanted to struggle and bark, but she couldn't do either.

'Don't worry, Girl,' she heard a voice whisper. 'You didn't want to stay there, did you? You and I are going to have a little adventure.'

She recognised the voice at once. It was that man, Chills.

Chapter 2

Girl spent the rest of the night hidden in the bag Chills had thrown over her head. She couldn't tell where she was, but she could smell salt water.

She knew it was morning when she heard the seagulls making a racket, but it felt a long time later that Chills opened the bag and gave her a big grin.

'Now you stay quiet,' he warned, putting his finger to his lips. 'No barking, no growling and definitely no weeing in my bag!'

He closed the bag again as Girl heard another voice say, 'Ready, Chillsy?' She recognised one of the voices from the previous night.

'Hi, Beakie; yeah, I'm ready,' Chills said, and Girl felt the bag being lifted.

'Cripes, what have you got in there? The kitchen sink?'

Chills laughed. 'A woodwork project. For my spare time. Come on.'

Girl felt him hoist the bag over his shoulder. The single coin in her belly shifted and clanked, but it seemed no one noticed. She was a little afraid. She wanted an adventure, but where was Chills taking her? How would Carol find her when she came back to collect her from outside the supermarket?

Girl knew they had stepped outdoors when the sounds suddenly became louder. There were all sorts of interesting smells too: diesel oil and chips frying and fairy floss. Girl thought she must be near the Hobart docks. She wished she could see outside.

After a long walk, Chills put the bag down gently. The noises had changed and Girl could hear a babble of excited voices, footsteps and the roar of machinery. The smell of diesel was very strong. She could feel Chills's ankle pressed against her back and she was glad he was close by.

'You taking that on board?' a man asked.

'Sure am,' Chills said.

'It's a bit big. You should have sent it in cargo. What's in it?'

'A woodwork project,' Chills said. 'It's not heavy.'

The bag shifted as the man picked up the handles

to test the weight. Girl heard him grunt and then put it down and walk away.

'Chillsy! How's it going? I heard you were coming down this season.' It was a woman's voice. *She sounds friendly*, Girl thought, and listened more closely.

'Kaboom — great to see you,' Chills said. He lowered his voice so that Girl could hardly hear him. 'Hey, check this out.' He unzipped the bag a little and a slice of light shone into Girl's hiding place.

She saw Kaboom's face peering down at her, looking puzzled. 'What on earth's that?'

'A Guide Dog.'

'Did you steal it, Chills?'

'No! She's going to try fundraising in a new place, that's all. I'll bring her back.'

'You'd better,' Kaboom said. 'Don't let her scare the penguins.'

While Chills and Kaboom were talking, Girl took the chance to try and see her surroundings. Behind them was a huge blur of orange. Girl looked more carefully. It was an enormous ship sitting at the dock. Every inch of it was painted in the same bright colour.

A deep horn blew a blast that echoed over the docks and set all the birds squawking.

'Time to board,' Chills said. 'Don't tell anyone yet. She's a surprise.'

He closed the zip of the bag. Girl felt him hoist it to his shoulder again and the coin clattered around her insides. She'd only managed to collect one so far. She wasn't doing a very good job.

Chills climbed up steep steps and Girl's bag banged from side to side on the railings. 'Sorry, Girl,' he said.

'Who are you calling Girl?' a gruff voice said from behind.

'Not you,' Chills said.

'Good. Aren't you one of the chicken chasers?'

'Yeah. I'm Chills and this is Beakie. We're going out to Bechervaise Island.'

'Cool. Watching chicken chasers catch penguins is the best summer sport around. I'm Wreck, the dieso.'

'What's a dieso?' Beakie asked, which was just what Girl was wondering.

'A diesel mechanic is the god of light and machinery on station,' Chills said. 'We can't live without them, so be nice.'

Girl's head was spinning. What was a chicken chaser, and why was a dieso the god of light and machinery? It was all very confusing.

More stairs, more corridors, muffled voices. Chills kept knocking the bag against the walls and muttering, 'Sorry, sorry,' as he squeezed past people. There was so much noise! When he finally put down the bag, Girl could feel a roar beneath her feet that made the coin in her belly rattle. The horn blasted again, this time much louder and closer.

Voices echoed down the corridor. 'We're off!'

Chills patted Girl through the bag. 'You'll have to stay here for now. But don't worry, I'll let you out soon. You wouldn't want to go all the way to Antarctica without seeing a few sights, would you?'

She heard his footsteps walking away. The big orange ship was shuddering harder and harder and the voices had all disappeared. She could feel the water churning beneath them. She was going to Antarctica!

Chapter 3

It was a long time before Chills came back. The ship had set off smoothly enough, but after a few hours Girl felt it start to roll slightly from side to side. She could hear the water swishing underneath them. She wished she could see something. It didn't feel like much of an adventure being zipped into a dark bag while everyone else was outside.

She'd started to feel quite sorry for herself when Chills finally unzipped the bag and lifted her out.

'There there, Girl,' he said softly. 'Sorry you have to stay in here for a while.'

He looked around the cabin, which was strewn with bags, and frowned. 'I hope Beakie gets his unpacking done soon. There's not room to swing a cat in here.' Then he looked at Girl and laughed. 'Or a dog!' He lifted her up to the top bunk. 'You can watch things from up there while I unpack.'

Girl looked around the cabin. It was snug, with four bunks, a few cupboards, a desk and a door leading into a bathroom. Through a round porthole she could see waves rolling past outside. Chills was busily unzipping his other bags and packing things away into drawers and cupboards.

'Yo!' A young-looking man with a large nose and curly hair bounced into the cabin. He slapped Chills on the back. 'On the way at last. That was cool.'

'Better get your stuff stowed, Beakie,' Chills said. 'Weather report says we could have a rough night and everything has to be unpacked for safety.'

'Sure.' Beakie looked around. He caught sight of Girl on the upper bunk and jumped. 'What the hell is that?'

'*That* is Davis Station's new dog,' Chills said.

'What's it called?'

Chills lifted Girl down from the bunk and put her on the floor. 'She hasn't got a name yet. Nameless dog, meet Beakie your cabin mate. You're both first-timers down south.'

Beakie gave Girl a firm pat. 'The pleasure is all mine, madam,' he said, bowing. 'But you'll have to hop off my bunk for a while so I can unpack.'

'I'm going on deck — I'll take her with me,' Chills said. He looked down at Girl. 'Want to come and have a look around?'

Of course I do, Girl thought.

Chills picked her up, tucked her under his arm and tried to drape his jacket over her. It didn't quite close around her, but she was partly covered. He went to the door of his cabin, looked up and down the corridor, then stepped out and tiptoed along the corridor. He pulled open a heavy door that opened into a stairwell, clanked up a flight of stairs and opened another heavy door at the top.

As soon as he stepped outside, Girl felt a rush of wind in her face. It was dark on the deck and Chills carried her across a large, open space to the railing at the back of the ship. The wake spread out like a long white ribbon behind them.

'Welcome to the *Aurora Australis*,' Chills said to her. 'The icebreaker that takes us all the way to Antarctica. And this is the helideck, where the helicopters land.'

A voice came out of the darkness, startling them both. 'Chills, it's one thing to talk to the huskies and the penguins, but be careful about talking to a plastic dog.'

'She's not plastic, Kaboom, she's fibreglass, actually,' Chills said. 'What are you doing out here?'

'Same as you, saying goodbye,' Kaboom said. 'Thinking about all the people I'm going to miss. I wish I could bring my dog with me, but I won't see her for ages.'

'Are you down for winter this time?' Chills asked.

'Yes, a full year,' Kaboom said. 'Us weather observers have to do summer and winter now. You?'

'Just the summer for me,' Chills said. 'The Adélies are all gone by winter. I wish I was studying emperor penguins. Winter is when they get really interesting.'

'And the dog?'

Girl wondered what Chills was going to say. She hadn't thought about how long she might be away.

Chills shrugged. 'She's in for the Antarctic summer now. Did you know they're bringing out the last husky team at the end of the season? Dogs aren't allowed in Antarctica any more. Maybe she'll want to stay for winter too. I guess she can stay as long as she wants.'

He looked down at her and smiled. 'Hey! That's a good Antarctic name for her. Stay. What do you think, Girl? Do you want to be Stay? Do you want to stay with me?'

Girl could see the clouds rushing overhead and from time to time brilliant stars shone through. No one had given her a name before, everyone had just called her Girl. And no one had ever asked her to stay with them.

I like it, she thought. Stay was a good name for a Labrador.

'That's settled then,' Chills said. 'Stay. Now, Kaboom, is it true there's going to be a big blow tonight?'

Kaboom laughed. 'Oh, yes,' she said. 'A nice storm to welcome us to the Southern Ocean. Make sure Stay is strapped in good and tight. We're going to rock and roll.'

'I'd best be getting downstairs,' Chills said. 'Good night, Kaboom.'

'Night, Chills; night, Stay,' Kaboom said.

A gust of wind spattered them with salt spray as they crossed the helideck. Girl felt the droplets on her face, cold and strange. Chills pushed open the door and carried her inside. As he headed back to the cabin, she tried out her new name. She wasn't Girl any more. She was Stay. It seemed like they all had strange names down here and now she had one too. She fitted in.

Chills wedged her between the bottom bunks and strapped her down. She was glad, as she could feel the ship rolling more strongly. Beakie was already in bed and he just groaned when Chills wished him good night.

'Good night, Stay,' Chills whispered, so softly that Beakie couldn't hear.

Good night, Chills, Stay thought.

It wasn't long before she heard him start to snore, and a little while later the wind picked up outside and the waves began to crash. She was nearly asleep when she remembered what Chills had said just before he gave her a new name. She'd be gone for the whole of the summer and perhaps the whole of the winter too. It wasn't just a week or two. It might be a year.

It was a very long time to stay away.

Chapter 4

Stay woke with a jolt. It was so dark she thought for a moment she was back inside Chills's bag. The ship was rising up-up-up over the waves, then diving down-down-down the other side. It landed in the troughs with a crash that made everything shudder. The wind whistled past the porthole. Beakie was groaning and Chills wasn't snoring any more. Stay reckoned that he was awake too.

She was wedged firmly between the bunks, but with every roll of the ship the coin clunked and clattered around her insides till she wished she had no coin in there at all. For once she was quite glad she wasn't a real dog. She didn't think Jet would have liked this.

Thinking of Jet was a good distraction from the storm blowing outside and Stay remembered the long talk they'd had back in Hobart. Although she had been fundraising for so long that her paint was scratched and faded, Stay had never met a real Guide Dog. But Carol had come to pick her up from the factory where Stay had just been repainted and had taken her home for the night. She'd put Stay next to Jet's basket by the fire, and Stay and Jet had talked for hours.

Jet told her he'd lived with a family for the first year of his life and then had left them to go to Guide Dog training school.

Didn't you miss them? Stay asked him.

Jet's big brown eyes looked sad. *Of course. The three little girls in that family loved me and I loved them. But I always knew I was going to be a Guide Dog. I couldn't wait to start my training.*

What exactly does a Guide Dog do? Stay asked curiously.

Jet looked important. *Our job is to help blind people move around safely. We learn how to help them cross the road, go up and down stairs and get around obstacles.*

Can you really do all that? Stay asked, impressed.

Yes. I'm fully trained and I've graduated from Guide Dog school. I'm staying with Carol until I'm matched with my new owner.

What an exciting life you'll have, Stay said. *All I do is stay still and hope people put money in my head.*

Jet turned around in his basket a few times and then settled himself down. *But you're a Labrador! Don't you know what that means?*

No.

Labradors love to serve humans. It's in our nature. We used to be bird-retrieving dogs for hunters.

Stay thought that retrieving birds sounded like great fun. She loved birds. *So?*

We know how to influence our humans. If we feel something very strongly, we can make them feel it too, so we can usually get them to do what we want.

Stay felt like she was sitting up straighter. *Really?*

Yes, really. Jet crossed his paws. *It's easier with your owner, but it works with other humans too. You should try it.*

How? Stay asked. *I'm not a real dog.*

Jet lifted his muzzle and looked at her. *You've got Labrador eyes. If you want a human to do something, look at them hard and send a picture of what you want to their minds. That's why dogs like you are used to collect money. People look at you and remember how beautiful Labradors are. You make them want to give money to help the Guide Dogs.*

I'll try. Stay felt doubtful.

You'll be great. Just remember. Look them in the eyes and think hard about what you want.

The ship rolled sharply to one side, bringing Stay back to the present moment. She was on her way to Antarctica! She'd wanted an adventure, and Chills had come back to take her on one. She'd looked at him hard and sent a picture to his mind, and he had understood. Jet had been right. She could influence people.

There was a crash and a thump next to her. Chills had rolled out of his bunk and was on the floor. He groaned.

'You OK?' Beakie asked from the upper bunk.

'Guess so,' Chills said. 'You?'

'Bit crook, mate.'

'I'm a bit queasy too. Think I'll stay on the floor.'

Chills reached up and pulled the quilt off his bunk. He slid closer to her and tucked his arm through her leg. 'Good girl,' he murmured.

'Are you talking to that dog again?' Beakie croaked.

'Oh, shut up,' Chills muttered. He put his head down near Stay's feet and pulled the quilt over him. 'Stay still, eh?' he whispered. 'Everything else is moving too much.'

Sure thing, Stay thought. She braced herself. When the ship went up-up-up, she kept firm and steady. Chills locked his elbow around her leg and held on tight.

Gradually the storm eased. Chills's grip on her leg relaxed and he started snoring. Up in the top bunk Beakie groaned every now and then, but eventually he became quiet too. Stay kept awake, watching over Chills. She was still awake when the cabin slowly began to get brighter.

At full daylight there was a bang at the door. 'Rise and shine!' It was Kaboom's voice, sounding merry. She pushed the door open and came in, followed by another woman.

'How was your first night at sea?' Kaboom asked.

Beakie gave another groan and rolled over away from the light. Chills raised his head and rubbed his eyes. 'Awful,' he said. 'I always forget how horrible it feels.'

'You'll be right,' Kaboom said cheerfully. 'Breakfast is on. Scrambled eggs and bacon will fix seasickness.'

Beakie and Chills both groaned in unison and Chills pulled the quilt over his head.

'This is Gina,' Kaboom said. 'It's her first time down too, Beakie. She's working on that new laser program for summer. What's it called, Gina?'

'LIDAR,' Gina said. 'Light Detection and Ranging instrument. It beams a laser into the upper atmosphere. We're researching the hole in the ozone layer and climate change.'

'Morning, Laser,' Chills muttered. Beakie didn't say anything.

Stay looked over at Kaboom. There wouldn't be many adventures happening in the cabin today, but Kaboom looked like she was ready for anything. Stay concentrated on her.

'I don't suppose anyone wants to come up to the Bridge with us?' Kaboom said.

'Nuh-uh,' Chills muttered.

'What about you, Stay?' Kaboom asked. 'Want to come and see the great Southern Ocean?'

Oh, yes! Stay thought.

'I want her to stay here,' Chills said. 'She's meant to be a surprise.'

'Don't worry,' Kaboom said. 'Nearly everyone's sick in bed. No one will see her.'

Kaboom stepped over Chills, picked up Stay and tucked her under one arm. 'See you later, guys. I'll ask someone to bring you a cup of tea.'

'What about the Boss?' Stay heard Chills ask as Kaboom carried her to the corridor.

Kaboom didn't answer him. 'Seasick people are boring, aren't they?' she said to Stay. 'Don't worry, I never get seasick.' She looked over at the other woman, who was waiting by the door. 'This is Stay,' she said. 'Stay, this is Laser.'

'A nickname already?' Laser asked.

'Laser's pretty good: you should be happy. One guy last year had to live with "Scumbag" all winter and one of the girls got "Slumpy".'

'Why did you get called Kaboom?' Laser asked.

'On station I have to let off a weather balloon twice every day,' Kaboom said. 'It's filled with hydrogen. Which is explosive ...'

'Oh,' Laser said.

They started down the corridor. The boat was rolling so much that they moved from side to side in a one-two-three one-two-three step like a waltz.

'After we've been to the Bridge, let's go looking for albatrosses,' Kaboom said.

Stay felt a rush of excitement. She remembered seeing albatrosses on the television, as part of that program about Antarctica. They were some of the biggest birds in the world. Would she really be lucky enough to see one?

Chapter 5

The Bridge of the *Aurora Australis* was huge. A row of windows ran all the way across the front and through them Stay could see the prow of the ship and the cargo hold on the forward deck. There was a wide instrument panel and, in front of it, a tall chair with a fur-covered seat was bolted to the floor.

Kaboom put Stay down on the ledge that ran around the windows. The Southern Ocean stretched out in every direction. The ship climbed up over the waves and then crashed down between them, sending up a spray of white water. Small birds darted and zipped around the ship. Stay watched them intently.

'Down for another season then?' a man's voice said behind them.

'Hello, Boss,' Kaboom said. 'Yep, I'm back. Ship's very quiet this morning.'

Stay heard a chuckle. 'We had a couple of forty-degree rolls last night. No one's got their sea legs yet. They're all still in bed.'

'Luckily I never get seasick,' Kaboom said. 'This is Laser. Looks like she's got a strong stomach too. Laser, this is the Boss.'

'Morning, Boss,' Laser said. 'Great ship you've got.'

'She's a beauty, isn't she?' said the Boss. 'Specially built for Antarctica.'

'Have you seen any albatrosses yet?' Laser asked.

'Just the cape petrels,' the man said. Then there was a pause that would have made the fur rise on Stay's neck if it could have. 'What is that?' she heard him ask in an ominous voice.

Kaboom turned Stay around to face him. 'Boss, meet Stay. Stay, meet the Boss. Isn't she cute?'

The Boss looked her up and down. Stay wished she could jump down from the ledge and put her tail between her legs. He radiated disapproval.

'What's a Guide Dog doing on board?'

'Chills brought her,' Kaboom said. 'She won't be any harm.'

The Boss glared at Stay. 'We treat stowaways very seriously. Might have to throw it overboard.'

'Stay is a she,' Kaboom said, picking her up and holding her close. 'I'll see you later, Boss.'

Kaboom carried Stay off the Bridge and into the stairwell, followed by Laser.

'He was joking, wasn't he?' Laser asked.

'Of course,' Kaboom said. 'He just likes to kid around.'

Stay wasn't so sure. She'd tried looking into the Boss's eyes and they'd been very cold indeed. She didn't think he was a man who could be influenced by a Labrador's feelings. She was scared of him.

'Let's go on the helideck and look for albatrosses,' Kaboom said.

Kaboom led the way through a maze of stairwells and corridors and eventually shoved open a heavy external door. A splash of water hit the three of them in the face. The *Aurora Australis* was bucking like a horse and spray was flying everywhere.

'This looks dangerous,' Laser said, hanging on to the doorframe.

'You'll be fine,' Kaboom said. 'Come on.' She scrambled out of the door and across to the railings, hugging Stay close. Little brown-and-white birds flew around the ship, floating on the wind and looking as though they enjoyed the rough weather.

'Look at that!'

Stay stared in the direction Kaboom was looking. It was hard to see through the flying spray and up-

and-down movement of the waves, but she caught a glimpse of something that looked far too big to be a bird.

'Wow,' Laser said. 'What is it?'

'A wandering albatross,' Kaboom said. 'There you go, Laser. It's good luck to see one.'

The ship climbed over a wave and the bird swooped close to them. Stay had a clear view of its enormous wingspan. It skimmed so close to the water that she was sure it would be swallowed by a wave, but it rose up a little as the crest came crashing towards it, and flew over the top of the rolling white water.

'How beautiful,' Kaboom said. 'Do you know, Laser, they can fly for a whole year without landing on the ground?'

Another big wave smashed into the side of the ship and drenched them with spray. Kaboom laughed. 'We'd better get inside, or we might end up overboard.'

'Can I carry Stay?' Laser asked.

'Sure,' Kaboom said. 'She gets a bit heavy after a while.'

Kaboom led the way back to Chills's cabin and knocked on the door. When they went inside, Chills was sitting up in his bunk, eating dry biscuits.

'There you are!' he said as Laser put Stay down on the floor. 'I was worried you might run off with her.'

'The thought occurred to me,' Kaboom said. 'It's funny how you find yourself talking to her, isn't it?'

From his bunk, Beakie grunted. 'It's a bad sign when you're talking to the toys at the *start* of your time in Antarctica.'

'She's not a toy!' Chills and Kaboom said together.

'What is she then?'

All four of them regarded her. If she'd been a real dog, Stay would have wagged her tail. As it was, all she could do was look them in the eye and hope.

'She's ... a mascot?' Laser said.

'A buddy?' Kaboom added.

'A dog,' Chills said firmly. 'The only kind we're allowed to have in Antarctica after this season. So we have to treat her like a real dog.'

'Don't say that to the Boss,' Kaboom said. 'He made a joke about her being a stowaway and said he'd throw her overboard.'

'What?!' Chills turned to look at Stay, and she sent him a thought to keep her out of the Boss's way. 'I think we need to keep her hidden,' he said slowly.

'Oh, don't be silly, he was only kidding,' Kaboom said. 'I think he's worried that you've pinched her from the Royal Guide Dogs.'

'You never know when a captain's kidding,' Beakie grunted.

'Kaboom, go away,' Chills said.

'Why?' Kaboom looked hurt. Stay wished she could give her a lick.

'I'm going to put Stay somewhere safe and it's best you don't know where. Then the Boss can't get it out of you. Now go, both of you!'

Kaboom and Laser went out of the room without another word. Chills hopped up from his bed and pulled on some clothes. He looked down at Stay. 'Now where are we going to hide you?'

Chapter 6

She was back in the black bag again. Chills carried her down the corridors and stairwells of the ship, occasionally knocking her against the walls.

'Is the coast clear?' she heard him whisper to Beakie.

'Yep. Quick!'

A heavy door opened and then closed behind them. Stay smelt a strong diesel scent. The roar of the engine was so loud it made her head ring.

Chills unzipped the top of the bag. 'All right, Stay? No one will look for you in the Engine Room.'

Stay could barely hear him over the racket. The Engine Room was long and narrow and covered in grease. A huge shaft was turning to drive the ship. Surely he wasn't going to leave her there?

'Where are you going to put it?' Beakie asked.

'Her! There's a spare parts cupboard. I'll zip her up in the bag and hide her there,' Chills said.

Please don't! Stay thought.

'I don't think that's a great idea,' Beakie said. 'If one of the crew finds her, they'll take her straight to the captain. Isn't there somewhere else?'

'Maybe you're right,' Chills said. 'Cookie might help us out. There's a huge storeroom under the Galley.'

'Come on, let's get out of here,' Beakie said. 'It's making me feel sick.'

Stay felt a wave of relief. She didn't mind when Chills zipped her in again and carried her through yet another maze of corridors and steps. The ship's layout was so complicated she wondered how anyone came to know their way around.

The diesel smell disappeared and was replaced by the much more pleasant aroma of food. Stay tried to distinguish the different smells. Raw onions. Potato peels. Mince. And something she was sure must be chocolate cake. Carol's kitchen had had the same kind of smells and Jet had told her all about chocolate cake, which he wasn't allowed to eat but always wanted.

'Psst! Cookie!' Chills hissed.

Stay heard footsteps coming towards them. 'Up and about at last, eh? It's too late for breakfast.'

'Can you help us? We've got something we need to hide.'

'What is it?' Cookie asked.

'Better you don't know. But can we put it in your storeroom somewhere?'

'I don't know, Chills — sounds like trouble to me,' Cookie said.

'Cross my heart, no trouble,' Chills said. 'It's a surprise for when we get to Davis.'

'OK,' Cookie said. 'Go through the kitchen and down the back steps to the storeroom. You can put it behind the flour.'

It took a lot of shoving and grunting for Chills and Beakie to move the flour sacks out of the way and put Stay behind them in her bag. There was more grunting as they pushed the sacks back in front of her and dusted off their hands with a brisk swishing sound.

'No one will find you there,' Chills said. 'Don't worry, Stay, it won't be for long.'

Stay thought that Chills's voice sounded a little sad and she wished he wasn't leaving her. He'd promised an adventure in Antarctica, but now she was shoved in the back of a storeroom inside a black bag surrounded by sacks of flour. It wasn't very adventurous.

She wondered if there was anyone else nearby that she could send thoughts to. Someone who might be a bit more fun.

Chapter 7

Time passed and Stay lost track of day and night. The ship rocked forwards and backwards and rolled from side to side. The bags of flour jammed into her side and felt like they were crushing her. Sometimes there were footsteps in the storeroom, but, though she concentrated hard, no one came looking for her. It was very boring.

She thought about Carol and Jet. By now, Carol probably knew Stay had been dognapped. She'd be worried. Jet might be worried too. What about all the puppies that were ready to go into school? Stay wasn't doing her job raising money to pay for their training. What would happen to the blind people who were waiting for Guide Dogs?

And I wasn't really dognapped, Stay thought. She'd looked Chills in the eyes and wished for an adventure. She couldn't blame him for taking her, but she was leaving her important work undone and she was worried about it. The more the boat rolled and pitched and tossed, the more worried she became. She was being carried further and further from Hobart and didn't know when she'd be back.

Stay was so preoccupied with her thoughts that she didn't notice when someone came into the storeroom and started shifting the sacks of flour. It wasn't until the person grabbed Stay's bag and tugged at it that she realised what was happening.

'What's this?' she heard a woman's voice murmur, and there was another tug at the bag. 'And what's it doing in with the flour?'

The bag slid across the floor and came to rest against a pair of legs. *Rip* went the zip and light flooded in. Stay had been in the dark for so long she would have blinked if she could.

'What on earth are you?'

The woman looking down at her in puzzlement was dressed in black-and-white checked pants and a black top. Her red hair was pulled back in a ponytail and she had a smudge of flour on one cheek.

Take me out of here, please, Stay thought.

The woman crouched down and pulled the sides of the bag down. 'You're rather cute, aren't you? I wonder if Cookie knows you're here.' She looked around and scratched her head. 'Better come on up to the Galley, I reckon.'

She hoisted Stay on her hip, grabbed a bag of flour with her other hand and clumped up the stairs to the Galley.

'Check this out,' she announced.

Everyone turned around. Stay could see half a dozen people dressed in the same kind of checked pants and black tops. Some were chopping, some cooking, some washing dishes.

'What the hell have you got there, Ranga?' Stay recognised Cookie's voice as he came striding towards them.

'Found her behind the flour,' Ranga said. 'Any idea where she came from?'

'A pretty good one, actually,' Cookie said. 'She's on the way to Davis.'

'Well, she'd better come to Neptune's blessing,' Ranga said. 'It's always good to give Neptune a bit of a surprise.'

Everyone in the kitchen giggled. Stay wondered what Neptune's blessing was.

'Back to work,' Cookie said. 'Everyone's out of bed today. A full house for dinner, and they'll all be hungry now the sea's calmer. Hop to it, people. And don't forget we've got to make Neptune's brew.'

Ranga placed Stay on the floor and took up a knife.

The kitchen became a flurry of activity, with everyone chopping, peeling, slicing and dicing. Stay sat quietly near Ranga, who was cutting up potatoes so fast that her hands were a blur.

Everyone else speeded up too, until Stay could hardly keep up with what they were doing. One person was stirring the soup, another was deep-frying chips, a third was slicing up the biggest pie Stay had ever seen, and another was setting out desserts on a bench. Stay could see ice-cream, blueberry tart, bread-and-butter pudding and poached pears. It looked like people on the *Aurora Australis* ate very well.

'Ranga!' Cookie strode down the kitchen. 'You got the short straw. Neptune duty!'

'Oh, no!' Ranga wailed. 'I did it last time.'

'Last time was a bit mild, I recall,' Cookie said. 'Make it really evil. Take the dog with you.'

'Fine, sir!' Ranga saluted and then poked her tongue out behind Cookie's back. 'Why do they always give me the worst jobs?' she asked Stay. She picked her up and clumped back downstairs to the storeroom.

Ranga set Stay on the bench before she opened the fridge, peered inside and started pulling out buckets and bowls. A strong smell filled the storeroom. Stay could see Ranga wrinkling her nose in disgust, but Stay thought it smelt wonderful.

'Week-old vegetable scraps ... check!' Ranga said, emptying the contents of a bowl into the big white bucket on the floor. 'Slops from Friday's dinner ... check! Out-of-date milk ... check!'

She stirred the bucketful of ingredients and glanced over at Stay. 'But not disgusting enough, according to Cookie. Let's see, what else can I mix in?'

She rummaged through the shelves. 'Vegemite ... always good. Peanut butter ... adds texture. Soy sauce?'

She straightened up. 'Ah, I forgot the main ingredient!' She went back to the fridge. 'Week-old fish guts ... check!'

The last ingredient smelt a bit strong even for Stay's liking, but in it went with everything else. Ranga stirred and then lifted the spoon, holding her nose with her fingers. The mixture was thick and sloppy and light brown in colour. Something told Stay that humans wouldn't find it so attractive.

As Ranga carried Stay and the bucket back into the kitchen, Stay could hear a strange distant roar that sounded like voices.

'Phew!' Cookie waved his hand in front of his face when Ranga put the bucket down. 'Smells like a good mix this time. The hordes are gathering in the Mess and Neptune's getting ready. Anyone in the kitchen crossing sixty degrees for the first time?'

Everyone put their heads down and chopped or stirred or scooped harder.

'Nemo, you're a newbie, aren't you?' Cookie said. 'Get out there. And take the dog too.'

The boy who'd been stirring the soup trudged over to Cookie. 'They never mentioned this in the apprenticeship agreement,' he said, picking up Stay.

'There's a lot that never gets mentioned about Antarctica,' Cookie said.

A sudden cheer rose from outside. 'Greetings, King Neptune!' Stay heard someone call.

'Out you go, son,' Cookie said to Nemo, and gave him a push. 'Be grateful it can only happen to you once.'

Nemo carried Stay out of the kitchen. The Mess was jammed with people. Stay had no idea there were so many on board. There must have been a hundred at least.

A very tall creature in a long blue velvet cloak was standing with his back to Stay. His hair was pure white and on his head was a gold crown. He held a bright red trident with three sharp-looking spikes.

'Come on, you slimy pollywogs,' he called.

There was a gasp in the room as Nemo and Stay came into sight: everyone stared.

'Stay!' She heard Chills call her name from somewhere in the crowd, but there was nothing she could do. The big man in the cloak turned around to see what the commotion was about. His skin was dark blue to match his cloak and his white beard hung down to his belly.

Nemo backed away and Stay would have run if she could, but Neptune waved his hand and another blue-skinned man, draped in fishnets and seashells, stepped forwards and grabbed Stay.

'What have we here?' Neptune boomed.

His assistant held Stay out for everyone to see. 'A dog, King Neptune.'

'A dog! And has it ever been south before?'

There was silence in the room.

'No? Then the dog goes first,' Neptune said.

'Wait!' Stay was grateful to hear Chills's voice and see him pushing forwards through the crowd. 'Her name is Stay. She's with me.'

'No problem,' Neptune said with a grim smile. 'We'll do you both together.'

'But … I've been south before,' Chills said. 'I've had Neptune's blessing.'

'Oh, come on, Chills!' a voice called out. 'Don't be a wuss.'

The crowd started a slow clap, and Chills shrugged and pulled off his jumper.

'Kneel before Neptune!' the assistant demanded.

He knelt. The assistant put Stay down on the floor next to him and together they faced Neptune.

'Hey — don't let that stuff get inside her!' Chills yelled as Neptune dipped a ladle into the bucket of slops that Ranga had prepared.

Stay felt a trickle of cold, gooey liquid run down her shoulder and the crowd started to cheer. She saw Neptune ladle the gloop from the bucket onto Chills's head and everyone began laughing. Neptune's helper stepped up and rubbed the slime hard into Chills's hair.

'I now pronounce you South Polar Sea Dogs!' Neptune boomed. 'Part of the great brotherhood of sailors who have crossed sixty degrees south.'

Chills grinned ruefully and tried to wipe the slime from his head and shoulders. Stay realised he was laughing. They were all laughing, even the ones who were going to face the same fate. Suddenly she didn't feel so bad. It was a game, that was all.

'Wait!' It was the captain's voice and Stay felt a shiver of fear. He came pushing through the crowd and stopped in front of Neptune.

'This dog is a stowaway,' he said. 'She doesn't belong to Chills. She belongs to the Royal Guide Dogs. She can't go to Antarctica. I'm taking her into custody.'

Chapter 8

Chills grabbed Stay and held her hard against his chest. He smelt of fish guts, vegetable scraps and Vegemite: an utterly delicious aroma that made Stay want to stay there forever.

'Stay is here on official business, Boss,' Chills said in a loud voice. 'She's fundraising.'

'How much money has she raised?' the Boss asked. He reached down and grabbed her. Chills's arms were so slimy that Stay slid out of them easily. The captain held her up high and shook her. The single coin in her insides rattled loudly.

'One coin!' the captain said. 'The Royal Guide Dogs won't be happy about that. Do you know how much money she'd be making if she was sitting outside a supermarket?'

Chills got to his feet. 'That's because we haven't started fundraising yet. Everyone who's getting Neptune's blessing today has to make a donation. Get your money out! Put your coins in Stay's head before you kneel!'

The captain put Stay back down. There was a lot of shuffling and scuffling in the room and Stay could see people reaching into their pockets. As each small group came up to receive Neptune's blessing, they put money into the slot in Stay's head. Then they knelt down in front of Neptune and were thoroughly slimed, to the raucous cheers of their shipmates. By the time everyone had finished, the whole Mess was covered in slime and Stay was heavy with coins.

'See?' Chills said to the captain with a smile. 'She's hard at work as an official Davis Station expeditioner. She'll raise far more money on this trip than she'd get at an ordinary old supermarket.'

A big cheer rose up around the room. 'Let her stay! Let her stay!' everyone chanted. Stay looked around in surprise. It sounded as though people liked having her around.

Then someone at the back called out: 'We can pay the dog for Neptune's revenge!'

An even bigger cheer rose up and Stay wondered what they were talking about.

'Ten dollars!' someone called, and there was a round of clapping. A man pushed forwards out of the crowd and put some folded-up notes into Stay's head. 'Twenty-five dollars!' a woman called, and followed suit. When someone yelled, 'Fifty dollars!' the cheering rose to a new level. Finally a big bearded man stamped forwards. 'One hundred dollars for the chance to slime Neptune!' he boomed. 'You'll have to take it on trust. It's up in my cabin.'

The cheering dropped to a whisper as the bearded man stood in front of Neptune. 'Now it's your turn,' he said.

'Don't hold back, Horse!' came a yell from the crowd. Someone brought a chair and King Neptune sat down heavily. Horse picked up the bucket of slops and raised it high. He slowly turned it and emptied the contents over Neptune's head, and the whole room went wild. Horse put the bucket down and rubbed the slime into Neptune's hair and beard, almost skidding over on the slippery floor.

People are very strange, thought Stay. But she didn't care. She was thrilled about how much money she'd raised for the Guide Dogs. She was nearly half full of coins, and there were lots of notes in there too. All those puppies waiting to be trained wouldn't have to wait so long.

Finally Horse was finished. Neptune got to his feet, bowed to everyone and limped out of the Mess, trailing slime behind him. There was a big round of applause as he disappeared.

'Dinner's in an hour!' Cookie yelled out. 'Remember, Neptune likes to turn off the hot water!'

There was a collective groan and everyone who'd been slimed made a rush for the door. The rest started to clean up with mops and buckets. Ranga knelt beside Stay with a wet cloth and a bucket of fresh water and wiped her clean again.

'I'll put her in the Window of Sin,' Cookie said. He bent down to pick her up. 'Phew, girl, you're heavy now,' he said, hoisting her in the air. 'What did Chills say her name was?'

'Stay,' Ranga said.

'Righteo, Stay,' Cookie said. 'I know just the spot for you.' He carried her over to the window that opened between the Mess and the Galley, where Stay had seen all the desserts being laid out earlier. One of the kitchen boys moved the bowls and trays around to make some space. Cookie placed Stay right in the middle of the desserts, between the bread-and-butter pudding and the blueberry tart.

'A coin for each dessert!' He laughed.

Everyone came back for dinner not long after. They had fresh clothes and wet hair and some of them still smelt faintly of Neptune's slime. A few were grumbling about the cold showers, but most were smiling and some gave Stay more coins before they helped themselves to dessert. As the coins clinked down and joined the growing pile inside her, Stay felt very pleased.

Until she looked up to see the Boss standing in front of her. He took a few scoops of blueberry tart and looked down at Stay, his forehead wrinkled. 'It's all very well to raise the money,' he said. 'But how's it going to get back to the Royal Guide Dogs?'

Stay felt a pang. It was true: she had no idea how to get the money back to Hobart and, until it was there, she wasn't really doing her job.

The Boss gave her a pat on the head. 'Perhaps you'd better come and stay with me for safekeeping. Cookie! Bring the dog up to the Bridge after dinner. That's an order.'

'Sure thing, Boss,' Cookie called out from the kitchen.

Stay didn't like the sound of that at all.

Chapter 9

Cookie and Nemo staggered up the five flights of steps between the Galley and the Bridge with Stay in their arms, groaning under her weight and stopping to rest several times.

'Where do you want her?' Cookie asked when they reached the Bridge.

'Right there,' the Boss said, gesturing at the instrument panel. There was an empty space next to the radar screen.

Cookie hoisted Stay into position. 'Must be a fortune in there,' he said, rubbing his shoulder muscles.

'Best she stays where I can keep an eye on her, in that case,' the Boss said. 'That money needs to be kept safe.'

Cookie shrugged. 'No one steals in Antarctica. There's nothing to spend money on anyway.'

'Can't be too careful,' the Boss said.

'Good night then,' Cookie said. 'I've got an early start.'

As Cookie and Nemo headed off, Stay looked out ahead of the ship. Snowflakes fluttered down and landed on the foredecks, covering the cargo containers. They must have come a long way while she'd been hidden in the storeroom — far from the spring days in Hobart.

The *Aurora Australis* steamed steadily ahead and, as it grew later, the last of the visitors to the Bridge gradually drifted away.

Stay saw the Boss look around the Bridge. The first mate was right over the other side, looking at some charts. 'Happy there?' the Boss asked her softly. 'You've got the best spot on the ship, girl. You can see everything. We'll be cracking through the sea ice tomorrow. You'd like to see that, wouldn't you?'

Yes, thought Stay.

'We mustn't let those expeditioners keep you in Antarctica,' he said. 'Believe me, you'll never get home again. I know what they're like. Stick with me up here, and I'll make sure you and your money get back to the Royal Guide Dogs.' He patted her on the head. 'Don't be scared of me. My bark's worse than my bite.' He looked around again. 'And don't tell them I was talking to you!'

Stay smiled to herself. He was certainly a lot friendlier when no one else was around. Then she thought of Chills and Beakie and Laser and Kaboom and Antarctica. Chills had promised her an adventure and she still longed for it. What should she do? Go to Antarctica with him, or return with the Boss to her job in Hobart, full of money for the Royal Guide Dogs? She wished she knew how to decide.

The two of them stared out at the ocean ahead of them. 'Big iceberg coming up over to starboard,' the Boss said. 'You know what? I never get sick of seeing them.'

Stay watched as the ship moved closer to the iceberg. It looked like an enormous dollop of ice-cream. Even in the gloomy evening light it seemed to shine. The section of it below the water was a beautiful pale green and the cracks down the side glowed a bright electric blue.

'The blue means the ice has broken off from a glacier,' the Boss said. 'Do you want to hear a poem about an iceberg?

'And now there came both mist and snow,
And it grew wondrous cold:
And ice, mast-high, came floating by,
As green as emerald.

'That's from a very old poem called "The Rime of the Ancient Mariner" by Samuel Taylor Coleridge, Stay. We see some wondrous sights up here on the Bridge. You might see a jade iceberg like the one in the poem if you're very lucky. Look — there's a humpback whale!'

Stay followed the direction the Boss was pointing. She glimpsed the arch of the whale's back and the mist from its blowhole. As it dived, it lifted its tail and she realised how big it really was.

Dusk was starting to fall. Stay knew it was very late and most people had probably gone to bed. The light outside was a deep blue and the water was so dark it looked black.

'Time to close the bird curtains,' the Boss called out, and the first mate pulled the curtains in front of the first row of instruments and computer screens, cutting the Bridge into two sections. The front section was almost dark, with just a little light spilling onto the instrument panel.

'If the birds see the light, they can get disoriented and fly into the windows,' the Boss said to Stay. He rubbed his hands together and looked down at the instrument panel. 'Minus three degrees outside. That's getting a little nippy, Stay.'

Stay agreed. She was glad to be on the Bridge, which was warm and cosy. She liked how the bird curtains shut off the light and made the room seem like its own little world in the middle of a vast, dark ocean.

It wasn't such a bad place to stay, for now at least. It sure beat hiding behind the flour bags. But she did wonder what Chills was doing.

Chapter 10

The *Aurora Australis* entered the pack ice, a belt of broken-up, melting sea ice and icebergs that surrounded Antarctica for hundreds of kilometres in every direction. Stay's spot on the instrument panel, under the Boss's watchful eye, looked like becoming her permanent home. She loved watching the sheets of sea ice cracking far out ahead of them under the weight of the ship's prow. Sometimes the ice was so thick that the *Aurora Australis* had to stop, back up and charge full steam ahead to break its way through.

They passed crabeater seals (who didn't eat crabs at all, but lived on krill) and little black-and-white Adélie penguins, who looked very surprised to see a giant orange metal ship bearing down on them, and ran off or swam away as fast as they could. Small white birds fluttered and darted around the ship; Stay learnt that they were snow petrels, and a sign that Antarctica wasn't far off. The nights had almost disappeared and although the sun set for a few hours, it never got really dark.

The Bridge was always busy. Everyone came up to watch their progress through the ice and spot animals and birds through the binoculars. People put coins into Stay every now and then and the weight of the money kept her firmly anchored to the instrument panel.

In the wee small hours of the night, after he'd made sure no one else was around, the Boss would talk to her quietly. He told her stories of things he'd seen at sea, like whales and giant squid, icebergs so big that they floated in the sea for years and were given names, and pirate fishing ships that operated outside the law. He told her about stars and the aurora australis, red and green waves of light in the sky also called the southern lights. Their ship was named after the lights, which could usually only be seen in the winter months. Stay loved hearing his stories.

Chills and his friends came onto the Bridge several times, but he seemed to be keeping his distance and Stay felt a bit hurt. Perhaps he'd changed his mind about taking her to Antarctica after all? Perhaps he'd lost interest in her, now that the continent was near and he had more exciting things on his mind.

She tried to vibe him to come over to her one evening on the Bridge. He was standing far away, talking to Kaboom and Laser. Stay thought he glanced over at her every now and then, but she couldn't be sure. She felt rather lonely, staring out at the ice as dusk fell. The ship was abuzz with excitement, with everyone talking about what they'd do when they got to Antarctica and how much they were looking forward to it.

Stay wished she was going with them. Travelling home again on the ship started to feel like a boring plan.

The Bridge gradually emptied out as people left to go to bed. Chills and the others left without a backward glance, laughing loudly at some joke as they shut the door behind them. The Boss sat up in the big chair for a couple of hours afterwards, steering the ship carefully through the pack ice and around the huge icebergs. Then he yawned and stretched and called over the second mate.

'Your shift,' he said. 'I'm turning in. It'll be a big day tomorrow getting into the station.'

'Night, Boss,' the second mate said. 'Sleep tight.'

He waited till the Boss had left, then changed the music to something with lots of electric guitar and drums. He hopped up in the chair and tapped his fingers in time on the armrest.

'Hey, Angus, how you doing?' Kaboom wandered onto the Bridge. It was very dark with the bird curtains closed and Stay could barely see her.

'Good. And you?' the second mate said.

'Great.' Kaboom went over to the stereo and turned the music up. She called over it, 'I've got to do some iceberg observations for Jamie and I don't know how to use the radar. Can you show me?'

'Sure,' the second mate said. He jumped down from the chair and took her over to the screen. 'This shows the direction we're going,' he said, pointing to the top of the screen. 'You can change it like this.'

As he pushed the buttons at the bottom of the screen, Stay heard a sound down near the ground behind her. Hands slid up and grabbed her legs. She couldn't see who they belonged to in the dark.

Thanks to the loud music, Angus didn't hear them. The hands tried to slide Stay backwards, but she was so heavy with money that she hardly moved.

There was a scuffle on the floor beside Stay. Angus, who was still talking to Kaboom, had his back to her and didn't notice.

'We'll have to pick her up,' someone whispered. Two figures, dressed in black, stood up silently, grabbed Stay's legs, heaved her off the instrument panel and put her on the ground. They crouched next to her and froze.

'If you click this button, you can change the range on the screen,' Angus said.

'Sorry, can you show me that again?' Kaboom asked.

'Now!' one of the figures whispered. They lifted Stay between them and staggered across the Bridge in the dark. They nearly got tangled in the bird curtain, but managed to push through it. In the light on the other side, Stay saw it was Chills and Beakie who were carrying her. She felt a rush of happiness. They weren't going to leave her to be sent home after all!

'Quick,' Chills hissed. He pushed open the door out of the Bridge and checked to see no one was in the corridor. 'Into the Met lab.'

They carried her through a nearby door, with a sign on it that said 'Meteorology', and put her down on the floor. Chills had a sack in his hand and Stay thought he was going to throw it over her head. But to her surprise he rolled her on her side and started to fiddle with the lock on her base.

Stay felt a rush of alarm. He was taking the money! The Boss had been right! She wished she could growl and show her teeth. That money was for the Guide Dogs. How dare he touch it?!

Chills managed to unlock the panel and coins began to trickle into the sack. He put his hand inside and started to scoop them even faster. Stay felt sick as they rolled out. The notes were the last to go — the money that had been paid to get revenge on Neptune. Horse's hundred dollars fluttered out at the end. She felt Chills snatch it and stuff it into the sack. With all her might she tried to send a thought to him.

Don't you steal that money!

She heard him jiggle the bag and give a satisfied chuckle at the sound of the coins chinking together. Then he picked up one coin and put it back into Stay before closing the panel on her base and turning her the right way up.

'An excellent haul,' he said. 'Now put her in the bag. I'll deal with this.'

Stay felt Beakie pulling the black bag over her head. He picked her up and she felt him open the door, then start carrying her down the stairs. She wanted to howl. How could they betray her like this?

Chapter 11

Beakie carried her a long way through the ship and Stay lost track of the staircases and corridors. They arrived at a place that clanked and echoed. It sounded like a large, open area, but Stay couldn't imagine where she was.

She heard lots of scuffling and clacking before Beakie laid her down on her side. She felt him pile a whole lot of heavy things on top of her. She wanted to struggle or to find some way to escape, but there was nothing she could do.

'See you later, Stay,' he said.

She heard a door slam nearby and then the distant sound of his footsteps disappearing.

Stay felt lonely. She had let herself be dognapped and now she'd let herself be robbed too. All that money was gone. How would she ever raise so much again? She'd thought Chills and Beakie were her friends. That

57

part hurt most of all. She'd trusted Chills, and it looked like she'd been wrong.

Jet had told her that Labradors were a trusting breed. *Too trusting*, Stay thought. She should have been more suspicious. Perhaps all along Chills and Beakie had been planning to rob her and then hide her so no one would find her before the ship headed home from Antarctica.

She tried to send a thought to the Boss to come and rescue her, but wherever she was on the ship, she couldn't sense humans nearby. *I won't even see Antarctica now*, she thought. She'd spend the rest of the voyage stuck inside a bag and when she did get back to Hobart, she wouldn't have any money to show for it. Nothing. Stay sank into misery.

Hours passed. Eventually Stay could sense the buzz of human excitement on the ship. She realised that the day of their arrival had begun and everyone was awake. This was the day they would crack through the sea ice to get as close as possible to Davis Station. The Boss had told her how he would push and push until the ship was firmly wedged into the fast ice, which was thick sea ice attached to the shore, so the cranes could unload the cargo containers over the ship's side straight onto the frozen ocean. Big trucks and machines from the station would then carry the containers to land, along with all the people. A fuel line would be connected from the ship to the tanks on shore and the *Aurora Australis* would pump out hundreds of thousands of litres of diesel fuel needed to run the station.

'It can take a week to resupply the station, or even more if anything goes wrong,' the Boss had told her. 'We have a thing called the A-factor, which means that in Antarctica something nearly always goes wrong.'

The Boss would notice she was gone, Stay knew, but this was his busiest time. Getting the ship wedged into the ice without breaking it up and making it unstable was a delicate and dangerous business. He'd need all his concentration to do it properly. He'd have no time to come looking for her.

Stay thought that they must be getting close to the station. The ship went *crunch-crackle-grumble-crack-crunch* forwards through the ice and stopped. It backed up with a heavy roar of engines and then moved forwards again. *Crunch-crackle-ram-crack-boom!*

The *Aurora Australis* stopped. They had arrived. They were in Antarctica. As hard as she could, Stay sent out a silent plea for anyone, anyone on the ship at all who might hear her.

Help me!

But no one heard.

The noises of cargo unloading went all day and all night. Stay imagined that she was blind. Without being able to see anything, her hearing became even more acute. She could picture the unloading process from the sounds that were magnified through the ship's hull.

Stay heard the big ship's crane groaning as it lifted the containers high in the air, swung them over the ship's side and lowered them to the ice. If she strained her ears, she could hear the sound of cracking and shifting in the ice when the heavy containers landed.

The trucks rumbled back and forth between the ship and the station. She heard excited laughter and talking as the passengers crowded at the top of the gangway and then made their way down. Stay heard the throb of the pump sending fuel through the long, flexible pipe and across to the shore. Very close to where she was hidden, she heard the *doof-doof-doof* of the helicopter taking off and landing, its blades beating rhythmically.

Sometimes, if it wasn't too noisy, she could hear the squawking of penguins and little splashing noises when they were swimming nearby. Antarctica sounded so interesting! Stay was terribly frustrated that she couldn't see it.

From the way the ship sounded more and more echoey, Stay realised that the resupply was almost finished. She could tell there were far fewer humans on board now — just the crew who would be taking the ship back to Hobart. The Boss had told her that the handful of people who'd spent winter in Antarctica would be coming back with them too. But compared with their trip down, the ship would be very quiet on the way home.

Stay moped in the darkness and thought mean thoughts about Chills and Beakie and even Kaboom, who'd seemed so nice and wasn't nice at all.

Everything went quiet and eventually Stay fell asleep.

Chapter 12

A sharp metallic *CLANG* jolted Stay awake. She was moving. She rocked from side to side. The single coin clattered and spun inside her until she had a funny feeling in her belly. She couldn't see anything, but it felt like she was being lifted into the air. Then she heard a familiar metallic groaning noise. It was the sound the crane made when it was lifting something heavy.

She must be inside something big that was being unloaded. Stay's heart leapt. Perhaps she *was* going to Antarctica! She hoped she was, and that she wasn't simply being shifted around the cargo hold to another spot.

The wind was whistling in the chains, and the rocking motion would have made a real dog seasick. She was going up-up-up. Then the movement of the crane halted and she was hanging, suspended in the air. She could faintly hear voices far below, but couldn't make out their words.

There was a jerk and she was moving again. This time it was down-down-down until she felt the crunch as she landed on the ice.

'OK! Get that Hägg unhooked and into shore ASAP!' a man's voice yelled. 'The wind's picking up. No more crane lifts today. Hurry up!'

Whatever a 'Hägg' was, Stay figured out that she was inside it. She heard the clatter of chains as the men unhooked the crane and then a door slammed close to her hiding spot. An engine roared into life right under her ear, giving her a fright. Then she started moving. *A Hägg must be some kind of vehicle*, Stay thought.

They crunched over the ice and then Stay heard the change in sounds. They were no longer on the sea ice — she could hear the sound of gravel beneath them. Why, they must be on Antarctica itself! She wished she could look out.

The driver parked the Hägg, turned off the engine and jumped out. Everything went quiet for a while and then Stay heard the door open.

'She's under there, unless someone found her,' a familiar voice said. Stay recognised Beakie.

There was a scuffle as he pulled back the baggage covering her. 'Aha!' he said. He ripped open the zip. 'There she is!'

Another pair of hands came pushing through. 'Show me!'

It was Chills, and Stay felt a rush of pleasure at the sound of his voice, followed immediately by a wave of anger. Chills had stolen her money and she was determined not to trust him again. She concentrated on sending him an angry thought.

'Phew,' Chills said. 'I was sure the Boss was going to find her. Come on, Stay.'

He pulled her out of the bag and gave her a pat. He was dressed for the cold, in a big heavy brown jacket with mittens, a beanie and rubber boots that clanked when he moved.

Stay hardened her heart. She wouldn't let herself feel close to him, not again. This time she'd be less trusting of humans like Chills.

'What are you going to do with her?' Beakie asked.

'I'm taking her out on the quad bike to wave goodbye to the ship,' Chills said. 'So the Boss knows she's staying here.'

'Be careful,' Beakie said. 'He might stop the ship and come back.'

'No way,' Chills said. 'Once the ship's broken out of the ice, she doesn't come back for anything.'

'Better hurry,' Beakie said. 'They've started the engines.'

'Meet you at the Last Husky afterwards. In the LQ?'

'What's the LQ? And the Last Husky?'

'Don't you know anything?' Chills said. 'The LQ is the Living Quarters and the Last Husky is the bar.'

Chills tucked Stay under his arm and backed out of the Hägg. Stay only had time to see that the Hägg was a bright red vehicle with tracks instead of wheels, before Chills was running towards a big square building. The ground was a mixture of dirt, rocks and half-melted dusty snow and the road was covered with frozen puddles. The station was scattered with bright, colourful buildings like giant blocks of Lego. It wasn't what Stay had imagined Antarctica would look like.

Chills wrenched open a heavy door and stamped his boots on the floor. He ran over to a row of quad bikes, and sat Stay on the back of one. He lashed her down, tying and pulling the knots so quickly that she could hardly see his hands moving. He jammed his gloves back on, pulled on a helmet and swung his leg over the bike. It started, and he warmed it up for a few minutes before letting out the throttle.

'Hang on, Stay!' he called over his shoulder, and they sped through the door and outside. They scooted through the station's ramshackle collection of buildings. In the distance she could see the ship slowly turning. Smoke was rising from its stack.

Chills and Stay bumped down a gravel road, across a muddy stretch and onto the flat sea ice. It was a pretty pale blue colour, and quite smooth and shiny. Chills accelerated and the quad bike sped over the ice in the direction of the ship. At the last minute he swung off to one side and they coasted to a stop. Stay could see streams of moisture coming out of his eyes from the wind.

'The Boss will be furious!' Chills said gleefully as he climbed off the bike and stood next to Stay, his arm across her back.

A whooshing noise came from the deck of the ship and Stay saw something fly up in the air. A moment later it popped like a firecracker and a glowing orange light started to drift slowly down towards the sea ice.

'That's the goodbye flare,' Chills said. 'They're not coming back now.'

He unlashed Stay from the back of the quad bike, raised her in the air above his head and started jumping up and down. 'There you go, Boss!' he yelled. 'We got her after all. She's staying here!'

Stay heard a deep, loud blast from the ship's horn. She could see tiny figures on the Bridge and one of them came out on the deck to stare.

'Aha!' Chills said. 'They've seen us. Give the Boss a wave, Stay.'

Stay remembered suddenly that the Boss had looked after her and promised to return her to the Royal Guide Dogs, while Chills had stolen her money and dognapped her twice. Once the ship left, she was stuck in Antarctica for months and she didn't know what had happened to the money she'd raised. She looked at the ship as it manoeuvred slowly around in a circle and felt a rush of homesickness. She didn't want to stay in Antarctica at all. She wanted to be sitting up on the Bridge with the Boss, full of money, on her way back to Hobart.

Stay looked around. Antarctica was huge. Ice and snow spread out all around them. The sky looked absolutely enormous, perhaps because she could see the horizon in every direction. Two rocky islands stood up out of the sea ice, one of them covered with thousands of penguins. A big brown bird flew over their heads and let out a hoarse cry before heading in the direction of the ship. It felt like a desolate place.

'He should have found the ransom note by now,' Chills said, lowering Stay to the ground.

Stay wondered what he meant.

'Deliver the takings to the Royal Guide Dogs or you'll never see Stay again,' Chills said, patting her head. 'You raised six hundred and thirty-three dollars and forty-five cents on the voyage down, Stay. It's on the way back

to Hobart in the ship. Let's see how much more you can raise over summer, hey?'

Stay stared up at him. He hadn't stolen the money after all. A warm feeling of relief started to spread through her. Six hundred and thirty-three dollars and forty-five cents on the way back to Hobart! She still had the whole summer in front of her. And Chills *hadn't* betrayed her.

Chills lifted Stay onto the back of the quad bike and started to tie her in place again. 'You'll have a fantastic time here. Lots of animals to meet, weird people to hang out with, places to see, things to do. It's the best place in the world.'

Stay looked out across the sea ice. The ship had turned completely around and was starting to move away from the station. For some reason the scene didn't look desolate any more. In fact, it was beautiful. Huge blue icebergs were scattered around the bay as if they'd been thrown there by some Antarctic giant and then frozen into place by the sea ice. The sun sparkled on the ice and in the distance Stay could see a line of black-and-white penguins marching along like toy soldiers.

'Party time,' Chills said, throwing his leg over the bike and starting the engine. 'Everyone will be thrilled that we outwitted the Boss and kidnapped you. You'll be the star of the show, Stay.'

He pressed his thumb to the throttle and the quad bike started to move across the ice. 'You're in for the adventure of your life,' he called over his shoulder.

Stay would have grinned if her mouth could move.

Chapter 13

A roar of voices rushed out when Chills opened the door to the LQ. A cold breeze had sprung up and it seemed everyone was inside. Chills hoisted Stay on his shoulder and carried her in.

Stay saw a confusing mob of faces, most of them with beards, turned towards her. Cheering broke out. 'Let her stay! Let her stay!' someone started chanting, and they all joined in, raising their glasses towards Stay and Chills.

'You got her!' Kaboom said, pushing her way through the crowd to Chills. 'Brilliant!'

'Beakie and I hid her in a Hägg,' Chills said. 'She came off the ship as part of cargo.'

'I bet the Boss isn't too happy.' Laser had come up to join them.

Chills laughed. 'He'll be furious. Let's hope he's forgotten by the time he comes back to pick us up.'

Kaboom shook her head. 'That man never forgets anything, Chills.'

After being hidden in the dark for so long, Stay was enjoying being high in the air on Chills's shoulder. She could see all the expeditioners crowded together in the bar for their welcome drinks. Through the window she glimpsed the frozen bay and the trail of broken ice where the ship had departed.

'Where are we going to put you?' Chills wondered aloud, looking around.

Somewhere nice and high, Stay thought. If she stayed on the ground in this crowd, the only thing she'd see would be legs. She wanted to see all the faces and enjoy the view of Antarctica out the window.

'Why not up on the bar?' Kaboom suggested. 'A good view from there. She can be the mascot of the Last Husky.'

'Good idea,' Chills said. He pushed through the crowd towards the bar. It seemed to take a long time. Everyone wanted to pat her. At last Chills placed Stay on the wooden ledge.

'Hey, Brewmaster, is it OK if she stays there?' he called to the man behind the bar. The man shrugged and smiled.

'Now I really need a drink,' Chills said. 'What's the station brew like this year?'

'Fantastic,' Kaboom said, making her way up behind. 'Can you get one for me and Laser too?'

'And for me!' Beakie said, pushing his way through the crowd to join them.

The Brewmaster poured out four drinks and they lifted their glasses and turned to face Stay.

'A toast to Stay,' Chills called out. 'For escaping the clutches of the Boss.'

'Cheers!' everyone said in unison, raised their glasses and drank.

'And don't forget to put in some money when you get a drink,' Beakie added.

There was some friendly laughter. 'Everything here is free, Beakie,' Chills said. 'But hopefully people will throw in a few coins for Stay.'

Stay looked around. So this was going to be her home. The LQ was cosy but comfortable, and seemed very warm. There were so many people that the babble of voices was nearly deafening and she stopped trying to listen to their conversations. She could smell dinner being prepared nearby and she thought it smelt like roast beef. She wondered where the food came from in Antarctica. She hadn't seen any plants and certainly no cows or chickens.

The roar of voices was a happy sound. The humans were all excited about starting their season in Antarctica and there was a big smile on every face. She looked down at Chills, Beakie, Kaboom and Laser, who were standing together, talking and laughing. *They're my friends*, Stay thought. She was glad she had them. The LQ was full of unfamiliar people and she knew it would take her a long time to remember all the names.

Suddenly the sound of a siren screeched through the bar, cutting through the voices and making everyone jump. Some people clapped their hands to their ears and everyone stopped talking.

'What's that?' Laser asked.

'Fire alarm,' Kaboom said. Stay thought she had gone pale.

A radio set near the door crackled into life. 'Attention! All station personnel! We have a fire in LQ. Fire crew immediately take up positions. All other personnel assemble at your muster point outside.'

'Oh my god!' Laser clutched Chills's arm. 'We haven't even been here a day! We could die.'

Stay could see fear on many faces. Some people put down their drinks and started towards the door.

'We'll be all right,' Chills said, but Stay thought even he sounded worried. 'I've got to run; I'm on the fire crew.'

'Me too,' Kaboom said. 'Let's go.'

They headed for the door. Beakie turned to Laser. 'Stick with me,' he said. 'We'll be OK.'

What about me? Stay thought. *Don't leave me here!*

The bar was emptying fast. Stay sent her thoughts towards any passing human as hard as she could, but no one took any notice. They were streaming out of the room, all with their backs to her. She had no chance to look anyone in the eye. Within a few minutes she was left stranded on the bar.

'Ah, they've all forgotten you, have they?' a big voice boomed behind her. She recognised the voice as belonging to Wreck, the dieso. She felt his heavy arm come over her shoulder.

'You'd better come with me then, eh?' he said.

Wreck tucked her under his arm and headed outside. People were milling around in confusion. The fire crew drove up in a red Hägg, jumped out and started working feverishly to unroll the hose.

A man stepped forwards. 'Are you ready, fire crew?' he yelled.

'Ready!' they called as the last kink rolled out of the hose. They were standing in a line holding it, poised to fight the fire.

The man looked at his watch. 'Eight minutes. Not good enough.'

What? Stay wondered.

'That was your first fire drill,' the man said.

A loud groan came from everyone and the fire crew straightened up from their crouching positions.

'I'm Smoky, your fire chief. Fire is one of the biggest dangers we face down here. You've got to respond instantly.'

Another man walked over to Smoky. 'That "fire drill" broke so many regulations I don't even know where to start,' he said.

Smoky shrugged. 'Sorry, Dux. But no one will forget it.'

Dux turned to everyone else. 'Hi, folks. For those who haven't met me, I'm Dux, the station leader. Smoky is right, you need to respond to a fire alarm instantly. Fire is a serious risk to our safety and survival. For the next drill, the fire crew needs to be faster and the rest of you stay in the LQ and take a roll call. We need to know ASAP if anyone is missing when there's a fire. Understood?'

'Yes, sir!' everyone chorused.

'OK, you can head back inside. Dinner's just about ready.'

Stay was starting to feel uncomfortable under Wreck's arm. He was holding her much too tightly and backing away, and she didn't like it. She looked through the crowd, hoping to see Chills. He was patting Laser on the back and Stay willed him with everything she had to look up.

It worked! He looked over in her direction just as Wreck was starting to turn.

'Hey!' Chills called, and began moving towards them. 'Where are you headed?'

Wreck started to walk faster. If Stay was a real dog, she would have pulled back hard on her lead. *Hurry up!* she thought in Chills's direction.

'Wait!' Chills called, breaking into a run. 'Hold on, Wreck.'

'You left her behind in a fire drill,' Wreck said over his shoulder. 'Too bad, mate. She's mine now. I've got a great spot for her in the machinery shop. Welded down, I reckon.'

'She is not yours!' Chills reached them and grabbed Stay's leg. 'Hand her over!'

Wreck pulled back, hanging on to Stay. Stay was in the middle of a tug-of-war, with two big men pulling hard. She could hear voices rising around them, some laughing and some yelling. She could feel that Wreck was stronger. He was pulling so hard that he was dragging Chills and Stay towards him.

Suddenly Stay felt Wreck slip. He'd reached a patch of slick ice on the track and his feet started scrabbling. Chills was dragged along by the weight until his feet reached the ice and slid. The tug-of-war was turning into a fight to stay upright, and they were all losing.

With one final skid Wreck went down, pulling Stay and Chills after him. They landed with a loud crack on the ice in a tangle of arms and legs. Lying underneath them, Stay wondered what had made the noise. She felt people pulling the two men up and as their weight lifted off, she saw Chills staring down at her in horror.

'Oh, no!' Chills cried. He knelt beside her and gathered her into his arms. 'Wreck, you idiot. Look what you've done!'

Stay looked up. She could see faces crowding around them, looking down at her. Something was terribly wrong.

Chapter 14

Stay sat on the table between Chills, Beakie, Laser and Kaboom as they all considered her. Laser had tears in her eyes and Chills looked furious.

Stay felt shaky. Her right leg had snapped and crushed in the fall and was dangling from her chest. It was a horrible feeling, as though she would tip over any minute. She was injured, and badly. What would happen to her now?

'Maybe we can glue her leg back in place?' Kaboom suggested, peering at it closely.

'I don't think so,' Chills said. 'It's ruined.'

'We should just cut it off,' Beakie said. 'It looks awful hanging there like that. Let's just remove it.'

'What, and leave her with a great big hole in her chest?' Chills snapped.

Stay looked at him in shock. Her purpose was to collect money. With a big hole in her chest, any money that was put into her could just fall out again. If that happened, what use was she?

'Chuck her in Warren,' someone said, walking past.

'Rack off!' Chills growled.

'What's Warren?' Laser asked.

'The incinerator,' Kaboom said.

The four of them stared at her. 'I don't think you can take her to the island like that,' Kaboom said.

Chills looked upset. 'I can't leave her here. She's my responsibility.'

Another man approached them and put his dinner down on the long table. 'Mind if I sit here?'

They all shook their heads. Stay checked out what he had on his plate as he started eating. The roast beef she'd smelt earlier, with roasted potatoes, pumpkin, gravy, peas. *Mmm. Smells good*, she thought. He had a big bowl of chocolate pudding with custard drizzled over the top for dessert. It looked like the station food was as good as the ship food.

'Going to fix her?' the man asked.

Laser shook her head. 'How? No one has fibreglass down here to make her a new leg. Her old one is crushed so we can't glue it back on. The best we can do is cut it off and put some duct tape over the hole, but that will look awful.'

The man looked over at Stay. 'I reckon I could make her a new leg. I brought some nice bits of Huon pine down with me to do some woodcarving over summer. I think I could set one in that socket. Won't look as good as new, but it'll do the trick.'

'Really?' Chills looked hopeful. 'Can you do it by tomorrow?'

The man shook his head. 'Nope. First few days on station are busy, and it'll take me a while to carve it so it looks like the other leg. Three or four days, I reckon.'

Chills slumped down in his seat. 'That's no good for me. I have to go to Mawson on the Twin Otter tomorrow so I can head out to Beche and start my research.'

'Oh, you're the chicken chaser, are you?' the man asked. 'I'm Bear.' He stretched out a hand and shook with Chills.

'Where does "Bear" come from?' Laser asked.

Bear grinned. 'I'm a plumber, so they started calling me "Pooh Bear". I prefer Bear.'

Kaboom looked at Chills. 'You don't have much choice, mate. I'll look after Stay until you get back.'

'But that's the whole season!' Chills said. 'I wanted to take her with me!'

'Never mind,' Laser said. 'She'll be Davis Station's mascot, instead of Beche's mascot. Anyway, she can collect money here, and you can take her back to Hobart at the end of the season.'

Stay felt as heavy-hearted as Chills looked. She liked Laser and Kaboom, but it was Chills who'd brought her to Antarctica, and he was her special friend. She wanted to go out on the island and spend the summer with Chills and Beakie and the penguins. It sounded fun. There'd be no one there who wanted to weld her to the floor, or throw her into Warren, or use her for a tug-of-war.

But Kaboom was right; Stay couldn't go anywhere with a big hole in her chest. There was no other choice: she'd have to say goodbye to Chills and stay at Davis.

She wondered if Jet had felt as sad as she was feeling right then, when he said goodbye to his first family.

Chapter 15

Bear put Stay up on the bench and spent a long time examining her crushed foreleg. He pulled out a small saw and began to cut it away. To distract herself, Stay thought about Chills. He'd left that morning with Beakie to fly to Mawson Station, one of the other Australian bases, in a little Twin Otter plane.

Stay had gone with the others to say goodbye at the airstrip, a long stretch of sea ice that had been smoothed over to make a flat, clear surface. It was a brilliant, sunny day, with a light breeze. The pilot was already inside, running through the pre-flight check, and the plane was ready to go.

'I was counting on you to call up a blizzard,' Chills said to Kaboom. 'Could have kept me here a few days until Stay was fixed. Is this the best you could do?'

Kaboom gave him a hug. 'I tried. Have a great season. Say hi to those Adélies for me.'

Chills hugged Laser and turned to Stay. *He looks self-conscious*, Stay thought, as if he was embarrassed to say goodbye. He patted her on the head.

'Oh, go on, give her a hug,' Kaboom said.

Chills crouched and wrapped his arms around Stay. She remembered he'd done the same thing the very first time they met, on the street in front of the supermarket in Hobart, and she felt warm and sad, all at once.

Beakie said goodbye to Kaboom and Laser and gave Stay a pat. Then he and Chills clambered into the plane and in a few minutes they had disappeared into the sky.

'There!' Bear said, breaking into Stay's thoughts and bringing her back to the present. 'We'll get that socket nice and smooth, ready for your new leg.'

Stay heard him open a drawer and rummage around inside. He came back holding a piece of brown paper and started rubbing the edges of the hole in her chest with it.

It was sandpaper. It felt awful and Stay wanted to growl. If she'd had real fur, it would have been standing on end. The sandpaper rasped and scraped and made her whole body feel restless and itchy. It was worse than having her leg sawn off.

'How's it going, Pooh Bear?'

Stay was relieved to hear Kaboom's voice.

Bear looked up and grinned. 'I feel like a dentist fixing a broken tooth.'

Stay shuddered at the same time as Kaboom pulled a face. 'Yuck, I hate the dentist,' she said. 'I had to have a filling down here last season. The doctor was the dentist and the cook was helping out!' She came closer and looked at Stay's chest.

Bear gave the hole a final rub with the sandpaper and stood back. 'There we go. All ready for the new leg.' He picked up a light-coloured block of wood from the bench.

Kaboom frowned. 'She'll look very odd with a square leg.'

'It won't be square. I'll carve her a leg just like the other one. It will take a little while, that's all.'

'Can I take her over to the Met office while you're working on it?' Kaboom asked. 'It's a bit lonely for her in here.'

Bear shook his head. 'I need her here for fitting and making sure the leg is the same as the other one. She can come over and live with you and the Met Fairies when she's done. As long as no one else gets her first.'

'What do you mean?'

'She's had a few visitors already. Quite the popular dog on station. Everyone thinks they've got the best spot for her.'

Stay saw Kaboom's face fall. 'But I'm looking after her for Chills. She belongs to him. Don't let anyone dognap her!'

'She might need a little more security,' Bear said. 'I've got a chain and a thumping big padlock so no one can get her out of here. She'll be safe. At least until her leg's fixed.'

'OK,' Kaboom said. 'Chain her up.' She patted Stay on the head. 'Goodbye, girl. See you soon.'

Bear laid the wood down on the bench. 'Sorry, old girl, but my shift's starting. I'll work on you again tonight.'

He looped the heavy chain through Stay's good leg and around the bench. She heard the click of the padlock closing and then the sound of his footsteps crossing the floor and the dull thud of the heavy door closing behind him.

The sound echoed through the machinery shop. It had a hard concrete floor, and hundreds of tools lined the walls. It smelt of grease and oil and timber and metal. It wasn't a bad smell. Rather interesting. Stay would have liked a chance to investigate more.

She was starting to get a little bored when the door opened again and some expeditioners came in.

'Here she is,' the first one said.

They clomped across the floor towards Stay. She didn't know them, though she remembered seeing them at a distance on the ship.

One of them picked up the chain and padlock and rattled it. 'She's locked up. How did they know we wanted to pinch her?'

'Everyone wants to pinch her,' the first one answered. 'She's the queen of the station.'

Stay quite liked hearing that and she sat up a little taller. It was surprising how often she found herself the centre of attention in Antarctica.

'For now,' another one said. 'They'll all get sick of her soon. By the end of the season, she'll be lying in a rubbish heap somewhere, forgotten. I bet you.'

'Done!' the first one said, and held out his hand to shake on it.

'You're an idiot,' the third one said. 'She's not even a real dog.'

'It just won't be the same without the huskies here,' the first one said. 'They're taking away our culture. It's not fair.'

They were all silent and Stay could feel that underneath their joking they were very sad. She wondered where the real dogs were. It would be fun to meet them. They could be her friends, like Jet had been. She wouldn't mind some dogs to talk to.

Perhaps these men would take her to the dogs? She looked at the short one, who'd said she was the queen of the station, and concentrated on him.

'It's a pity the huskies are all at Mawson,' he said after a while. 'I probably won't get across there to see them this season, and after that it'll be too late.'

One of the others slapped him on the shoulder. 'Tough luck, boyo. You'll never have the joy of sledging with the huskies — unless you go to Minnesota. I hear some of them are being taken there when they leave Antarctica.'

'You're kidding?'

'Nope. These dogs are celebrities. The last dogs in Antarctica. There'll be a huge crowd to welcome them back to Hobart. The old ones will retire to a life of luxury and the young ones will go to America and keep working.'

'I heard there's a litter of puppies,' the first one said.

'That's right, three new ones. Misty, Cobber and Frosty. Born to Cardiff and Cocoa.'

The third man scowled at Stay. 'And all we get here is the broken-down plastic dog. It's not fair!'

'Come on, you guys,' one said. 'Let's go. It's cold in here. Bye-bye, broken doggie.'

Stay wanted to lower her ears and drop her head. He didn't seem friendly at all, and she shivered a little.

The dogs were far away, at Mawson Station, where Chills and Beakie had gone on the plane. Chills was probably playing with those puppies right now. He'd forget her in a moment once he saw real dogs, especially pups.

Those men were right. She'd probably end up thrown in a corner on the scrap heap or chucked into Warren. Her luck had turned bad as soon as she'd landed on Antarctica, and there was no way to get home now.

Chapter 16

'Hold her still!'

Stay was lying upside down in a most undignified position, staring at the floor. She felt Kaboom take a tighter grip on her good leg. As if she could run away, even if she wanted to!

'OK, I'm setting the new leg in the socket,' Bear said. 'Brace yourself, Kaboom.'

Stay felt Kaboom's hands tense around her body. The heavy piece of wood scraped and wrenched and then slid into place. Bear wedged her new foot into the depression on the fibreglass platform that supported Stay. He gave it a tug. It fitted perfectly.

'I'll just put a little glue around the edge to make sure it doesn't move.' Stay felt the cold glue glugging around the socket where the new leg was fixed. Bear rubbed it carefully with a rag and gave her new leg a final polish. Then he turned her up the right way again, to Stay's relief. He carried her across the room to the bench and sat her up.

'There!' Kaboom said, and clapped her hands. 'You've done a fantastic job, Bear. It looks just like the other leg.'

Bear dusted his hands on his pants and grinned. 'No problem. It was fun to have a little project.'

'You're a good carver,' Kaboom said, looking closely at his handiwork. 'You've made an exact match. Even the paw is the same. Now can I take her over to the Met office?'

'Sure,' Bear said. 'I want to get started on carving something else anyway.'

He gave Stay a quick pat on the head and turned away. Stay had the feeling he was going to miss her, though he didn't say anything. He'd spent hours on her new leg. He liked to listen to guitar music while he was carving. 'The blues,' he'd told her. 'Best music in the world.' Stay had quite enjoyed the long hours of music as Bear chiselled and sanded.

Kaboom picked Stay up and headed out of the machinery shop. On the way through Stay noticed there were lots of people working. One section seemed to be for carpentry, another for mechanics and another for plumbing.

'I hope you don't mind leaving here,' Kaboom

said. 'It's a very cool place. People work on all sorts of interesting projects, especially over winter when they can't go outside as much. But the Met office is nice too. We have a view over the bay, and everyone drops in to ask us what the temperature will be. Plus we let off a weather balloon twice every day.'

She opened a heavy external door and the sunlight came blazing in, dazzling Stay for a moment. There was a rush of cold, crisp air as they stepped outside. Davis Station's colourful buildings looked even brighter than usual.

Kaboom set off down the road towards the frozen bay, treading carefully over the icy bits. Snow had fallen, melted and refrozen on the road, making a messy patchwork of icy mud. Stay felt a bit nervous about Kaboom slipping and dropping her — the last time she'd been dropped on the ice had been a disaster — but Kaboom knew the best way to get around the scary bits and they soon reached the Meteorology building. Kaboom pushed open another heavy door with her hip, stamped her feet on a metal grille just inside to remove the mud and snow, and carried Stay inside.

'Ta da!' she said when they reached the main office.

Three people sitting at desks looked up and when they saw Stay they jumped to their feet and came over to make a fuss.

'Oh, didn't he do a good job?' one of them said. 'Perfect match.'

'Stay, meet the Met Fairies,' Kaboom said. 'These are Rain and Hail, our weather forecasters, and this is Shine, the other weather observer with me. Shine and I have the important job of recording all the weather. The weather guessers are only here so they can tell the pilots if it's safe to fly.'

'Very funny,' Hail said. 'Is she staying here with us now?'

'Sure is,' Kaboom said. She looked around. 'How about we put her in front of the window? Then she'll have a great view outside, and people passing by can see her.'

They all agreed and shortly Stay was sitting in front of what felt like her own special window, looking out at the sea ice in front of Davis Station.

Shine looked at her watch. 'Shift change,' she said. 'Kaboom and Rain, you're on duty. Hail, want to come to the LQ?'

'Sure,' Hail said. 'Let's go.'

Kaboom started putting on a grey coat. 'Stay, you can watch from here. I'll be filling the big white weather balloon up with hydrogen and then letting it off just down there. It goes up into the atmosphere and takes readings on air pressure, temperature, humidity and wind speed.'

'Enough with the weather lesson and get going!' Shine said. 'You'll be late.'

'Give me a little wave when you see me, OK, girl?' Kaboom said.

'Kaboom, you're talking to the animals again,' Hail said. 'I'm getting worried about you.'

They all laughed as Kaboom put up the hood of her coat and went out the door, followed by Shine and Hail. While Stay waited for Kaboom to appear, she looked out at the bay. It really was very beautiful in front of the station. She knew that the two rocky islands rising up from the sea ice were Gardner Island and Anchorage Island. Out in the far distance she could see tiny black shapes moving in funny, uneven lines — penguins making their way out to the navy stripe of the open sea.

Kaboom came out of the Met building holding a white balloon about fifty times bigger than any balloon Stay had ever seen. She walked down away from the building to a clear space in the snow and looked up to see if Stay was watching. Stay felt a little thrill.

'Ah, there she is,' a voice said behind her. 'All nicely fixed up.'

Stay ignored the voice as Kaboom released the balloon and it sprang into the air, floating quickly upwards into the sky. It was amazing how fast it rose.

'Hi, Dux,' she heard Rain say. 'What brings you to Met today?'

'A certain dog,' he said.

The balloon had nearly disappeared. Kaboom was waving up at her and Stay wished she could wag her tail to show her that she'd seen it.

Then a big pair of hands took hold of her and lifted her up, away from the observation window.

'She's coming back up to the Last Husky,' Dux said, 'so everyone can enjoy her.'

'But Kaboom is looking after her!' Rain said. 'She belongs to Chills.'

'She belongs to the Royal Guide Dogs, I believe,' Dux said. 'I want her where I can keep an eye on her.'

Stay sent out a thought to Kaboom to hurry back upstairs. She liked the Met office and she'd be happy to stay there with Rain, Hail, Shine and Kaboom. The bar was too loud and too unpredictable. Everyone who wanted to dognap her could find her there. But she was too late.

'You're coming with me, old girl,' Dux said.

He tucked Stay under his arm, clomped down the stairs and headed outside before Kaboom reappeared. Like it or not, Stay was going back to the Last Husky.

Chapter 17

The wind whirled around the station and Stay could hear the sound of sleet hitting the windows like little stones. The sea ice was breaking up, and the strong wind was blowing it from the bay out to sea, revealing the water underneath. The miserable view from the LQ windows made her glad she was inside.

She didn't have that much else to be glad about. When Dux had brought her back to the LQ and put her up on the bar, he'd borrowed the big chain and padlock from Bear and locked her down tightly. No one could move her.

He patted her on the head. 'Stay there and make some money for the Royal Guide Dogs. No more mischief!'

It wasn't me who got into mischief! Stay thought, but he didn't seem to hear her thought the way Chills or Kaboom would have.

And so she stayed. Every evening after work was finished, most expeditioners gathered at the Last Husky to talk about their day over a couple of drinks. The Brewmaster was a popular person, Stay could see, and she learnt a lot about station life by listening in on the conversations.

At first she was very popular. Almost every day someone would stand next to her, take a photo, give her a pat, or talk about where they wanted to take her. One wanted her to come to a place called Platcha Hut for the weekend, a little orange field hut next to a fjord where a small group was going hiking and playing cards, a trip they called a jolly. Another wanted her to come over to the Greenstore and see how the year's supplies were packed and retrieved. A biologist wanted to take her looking for specimens on the sea bed in the bay once the ice melted, and Shine the weather observer kept talking about taking Stay to Woop Woop, which turned out to be an inland airstrip where the planes could land once the sea ice had broken up. Laser wanted Stay to visit the LIDAR building, from which they shot a laser beam up into the sky and examined something called polar mesospheric clouds.

But gradually, as they all settled in to their lives on station, people stopped noticing Stay. No one talked to her directly when they were with their friends, probably

96

because of being teased. They didn't even put money into her. No one used money in Antarctica, Stay had realised, and so they didn't carry it. All the meals were supplied in the Mess and the kitchen slushy always set out fruit and bread and biscuits for anyone needing snacks. There was a big store cupboard called Woolies, where they went for supplies like soap and shampoo and sunscreen. Nothing was for sale.

Everyone on station was busy, and when they finished a shift they were often tired. When Stay had first arrived, the sun had only dipped below the horizon in the middle of the night, creating just a few hours of twilight, with brilliant sunsets that turned the sky every shade from orange to purple. But now the sun didn't set at all — and wouldn't go down for another six weeks. People found it hard to sleep properly and they were sometimes snappy with each other. Stay heard them talk about having 'big eye', which meant not being able to sleep because it was too bright. She thought it was a silly saying — most people who couldn't sleep had slitty eyes, not big eyes.

Stay missed the way Chills had talked with her as if he could hear her thoughts. He *could* hear them, she was sure. Kaboom still talked to her like that, but she was busy with work and Stay didn't see her that much. She felt lonelier in the midst of that big crowd than she had even on all those long nights alone on the streets of Hobart. It didn't matter how hard she looked at someone and willed them to set her free, they couldn't. She was chained up. Trapped. And not an adventure in sight. When she heard that the elephant seals had arrived in their summer mud wallow down on the beach near the station, she couldn't rush out with everyone else to see them groaning and rolling around to loosen their old skins and let them peel off. The Adélie penguins over on Gardner Island were laying their eggs and, before the sea ice was completely gone, people hiked over to watch them. Stay couldn't do any of it.

When the big blizzard blew up and people were stuck inside, Stay daydreamed about Chills, far away on Bechervaise Island with another penguin colony. What did he do when there was a blizzard? Where did he sleep? What did he eat? There wouldn't be a Mess on the island, she was pretty sure of that. How did he have a shower? Or wash his clothes?

She sighed and looked out the windows again. She was bored, and she was pretty sure some of the humans in the bar were bored too. When they had to go out to reach another building, or to come back to the Living Quarters after work, they came in with their eyes streaming from the wind. The sea ice was almost gone, which meant no more driving across the frozen bay on quad bikes or Hägglunds, and no walking either. As the snow melted, the area around the station looked like a dirty pile of rocks and dust.

It was getting late and the expeditioners were starting to drift away towards bed. Someone was mopping the floor in the kitchen. Stay couldn't see who it was, but she guessed it was Kaboom taking her turn at slushy duty. Stay pricked her ears to hear the music. She knew that in return for doing a day's hard work, the kitchen slushy got to pick the music. Kaboom liked to listen to jazz, which always left Stay feeling sad.

The bar emptied out. Someone snapped off the lights and the gloomy grey glow of the blizzard outside settled over the room. Stay started to doze, trying to ignore the lonely sound of the wind whistling around the edge of the building.

Suddenly a scratching sound down on the ground jolted her awake.

'Can you see anyone?' she heard someone whisper.

'No. I'll keep lookout.'

Someone else was trying to dognap her. Stay didn't mind who it was — anything would have to be better than staying on the bar. But how would they get her out of the chain and padlock? Dux was the only one who had a key.

Stay couldn't recognise the dognappers. There were two people, both wearing balaclavas that covered their faces.

'Have you got it yet?' the one on the floor asked.

'Give me a second! I've only just found the padlock.' The first one snapped on a small torch, which cast a tiny pool of light on the padlock.

Stay recognised their voices. The one fiddling with the padlock was Laser, and the other one was Kaboom. Her friends were going to rescue her!

Laser had a ring of keys and she started trying to find one that fitted. Stay could feel the vibration coming up through the chain, and the little metallic sounds of the keys scraping against the padlock.

'I don't think the key is on this chain!' Laser whispered. 'Maybe he's hidden it somewhere else.'

Stay felt a rush of disappointment and willed them not to give up.

'You'll have to do it by feel,' Kaboom said. 'Be quiet. Dux has a nose for when something's going on.'

'Lucky he didn't notice we swiped his keys,' Laser said. She tried again. Stay wanted to squirm with impatience.

At last there was a click and she felt the lock spring open.

'Well done!' Kaboom said, coming close. They

unwrapped the chain and Kaboom lifted Stay off the bar. She gave her a quick hug. 'I missed you, Stay.'

'Where's the leg?' Laser asked.

What leg? Stay wondered.

Kaboom reached into her jacket and pulled something out. Stay realised it was her missing leg, crushed and dangling. She'd got so used to her new wooden leg that she'd nearly forgotten the old one; she shuddered at the sight of it. What were they going to do with it?

She watched as Laser wrapped the leg in the heavy chain, crisscrossing it until the leg was almost completely covered. She pulled the two ends together and padlocked them shut.

'Are you leaving a ransom note?' Laser asked.

'You bet,' Kaboom said. She pulled a folded piece of paper out of her pocket and read it aloud. *'Stay has gone. This is all you're getting. Don't come looking for her, or we'll cut off her other leg and send that.'* She tucked the note into the chain.

'Ooh, that's horrible,' Laser said. 'Don't worry, Stay, we don't mean it.'

Stay was very glad. But what were they going to do with her? She didn't really want to hide somewhere — she was sick of hiding. It'd be better to stay where she was than be put in a cupboard or under a bed.

'Come on!' Kaboom said. 'Let's get out of here before Dux comes back. Over to the helipad.'

'What, in the blizzard?' Laser asked.

'You bet. I'm putting her in the mailbag ready to go in the Squirrel. Can you smuggle those keys back into Dux's office?'

What on earth is a Squirrel and how do you get inside one? Stay wondered. It was another Antarctic mystery.

'I'm sorry, girl,' Kaboom said. She lifted up a mailbag and pulled it over Stay's head. Everything went dark.

Stay felt them carry her to the heavy outer door and open it. She heard Laser and Kaboom gasp as the blizzard hit them in the face and Stay felt the sleet rattling against the bag as they stepped outside.

'Hold on to the guide rope,' Kaboom said, the words whipped from her mouth by the wind. 'Keep one hand on it.'

Stay willed Kaboom to tell her where exactly she was going, but the wind must have been too strong. If Kaboom said anything, Stay couldn't hear it over the howl of the blizzard.

Chapter 18

Stay felt like she'd been hidden for days by the time the blizzard finally dropped. When the wind stopped shrieking, she heaved a sigh of relief. She had no way of knowing if it was day or night — though there was no such thing as day or night anyway, in the middle of the Antarctic summer when the sun never set. And however bright it might have been outside, it was dark inside the mailbag where Kaboom had hidden her.

Stay heard a loud thump. A door cracked open and a stream of cold air rushed in. She could hear voices and someone moving things around.

'About time we got the all clear,' a voice grumbled nearby. 'I've been waiting to take off for days!'

Stay recognised the deep voice of Nuts from the Last Husky. He was a tall man with black hair and a bushy black beard, who piloted one of the helicopters. Kaboom must have hidden Stay in the little office at the heliport, ready to go on the flight!

But where was she headed now? Some of the scientific teams who went out in the field to study rocks travelled by helicopter. Perhaps she'd be flying out to one of their camps for a visit?

'Remember, Nuts, you guys have got to be back from Mawson before dinner.'

It was Kaboom's voice and Stay felt a rush of excitement. Mawson! She was going to Mawson Station! The huskies lived at Mawson, and Chills was just nearby. Surely if she made it to Mawson she'd find a way out to him!

'Not fair,' Nuts grumbled. 'Can't even party with the Mawson dudes.'

'You know the rules,' Kaboom said. 'It's too windy for Squirrels to stay overnight there.'

'Yeah, yeah, so I hear,' Nuts said. 'Big winds flowing down off the plateau and all that. Very uncool. I've never been to Mawson and neither has Stretch. We wouldn't mind exploring.'

'Well, get moving!' Kaboom said. 'Have you got a mechanic with you?'

'Yeah, Bluey's coming along. He's going with Stretch in the other chopper. They're ready to go.'

Stay felt herself being picked up and realised Kaboom was carrying the mailbag outside.

'Got a bit of extra room?' Kaboom asked.

'I've got a spare front seat,' Nuts answered. 'Wanna come?'

'Love to, but I haven't got a day off till next week,' she said. 'This is a special delivery for Chills, next time someone goes out to Beche to drop off supplies or if he comes in to pick some up.'

Stay felt herself being passed up into the helicopter and put on the seat.

'Pretty big present,' Nuts said. 'What is it?'

'A surprise,' Kaboom said. 'And I mean that, Nuts. Don't open it. OK? And make sure no one else does either. I'd deliver it myself, but it can't wait.'

'It'll have to go on the front seat,' Nuts said. 'Can you buckle it in?'

Kaboom adjusted Stay so she was sitting on the seat facing forwards. Stay felt the seatbelt tighten over her chest.

'OK, we'd better get our skates on,' Nuts said.

'Travel safe.' Kaboom was talking to Nuts, but she patted the mailbag as she spoke and Stay knew she was talking to her as well.

'Always,' Nuts said. 'See ya!'

I'll miss you, Kaboom, Stay thought.

The door closed and Stay heard Nuts flick a series of switches and start up the engines. The blades began to turn, speeding up and making a *thud-thud* sound that she remembered hearing on the helideck of the ship. She could hear the other helicopter starting too.

'VLZ-Davis, this is Alpha-Foxtrot-Oscar,' Nuts said.

The radio crackled into life. 'Alpha-Foxtrot-Oscar, this is VLZ-Davis, reading you loud and clear.'

'Hi, dudes. Me and Sierra-Echo-Sierra are ready to take off for Mawson.'

'Safe flying, Alpha-Foxtrot-Oscar and Sierra-Echo-Sierra. Catch you for a drink later on.'

'Thanks, VLZ-Davis. Alpha-Foxtrot-Oscar out.'

The Squirrel vibrated and then suddenly Stay felt the machine rising into the air. She wished she could see out! It would have been incredible to see Davis Station from the air. With all her might she willed Nuts to turn around and free her from the mailbag, but he didn't seem to hear her thoughts. The helicopter rose higher and higher, then accelerated away from Davis and towards Mawson.

The flight settled into a steady hum, with a few bumps to keep things interesting. Stay could feel the coins rattling and vibrating inside her. There weren't as many of them as she'd accumulated on the ship, and she began to worry. If she did make it out to Bechervaise

Island with Chills, how would she raise any money for the Guide Dogs?

Perhaps it had been a mistake to stay in Antarctica at all. She really should have gone home on the ship with the Boss. She'd have been well and truly back in Hobart by now, spending her days and nights chained up outside a supermarket, willing people to put money inside her.

Stay sighed. Put like that, her old life didn't sound exciting. It sounded well behaved, the way a Labrador's life should. It sounded like what Jet would have done.

Then she thought harder. Hadn't Jet said something about adventures? And of course, he'd get to go on lots. Guide Dogs went everywhere with their owners, he'd told her. They went all sorts of places where no other dogs were allowed — on the bus, in restaurants, to the movies, to school: anywhere their owners needed to be. Other dogs were often left at home by themselves all day, Jet had said. Guide Dogs never were.

Stay felt a stab of homesickness. She missed having someone to talk to. Jet had been a great friend, though they'd only known each other a short time. He'd understood her.

The helicopter tilted, jolting Stay from her thoughts, and she felt it begin to drop. It was dizzying. The little machine felt like it was plummeting to the earth at full speed, nose first.

Stay felt a rush of terror. Was she going to be killed in a helicopter accident? She could hear the wind screaming past the windows and they seemed to be going faster and faster.

She tensed, waiting for the impact.

Chapter 19

The helicopter swooped up out of its dive so suddenly that Stay felt dizzy. It levelled, hovered and then gently touched down. She heard Nuts turn the engine off and the rotors slowly stop spinning. The second Squirrel landed nearby a few seconds later.

Nuts chuckled. 'Ah, I love having no passengers.'

Stay wondered if they'd arrived at Mawson. No matter what Kaboom thought, she couldn't stand being hidden in the mailbag and missing out on seeing everything. With all her might she willed Nuts to open the bag. This time he seemed to respond to her thoughts.

'Now I wonder what Kaboom is sending her boyfriend,' he murmured. She felt his hand on the bag, moving along her back and up to her head.

'No way!' Nuts said. 'Stay, is that you?'

He ripped open the bag, pulling it back from Stay's head, and gave a yelp that sounded quite dog-like.

'Cool!' he said, and grinned at her. 'A famous passenger! Dux will be spewing when he finds out you've gone.'

Stay looked outside to see Mawson Station, but all she could see was snow stretching in every direction and a few rocks. *Where are we?*

'Hey, dude, we're at Beaver Lake refuelling depot,' Nuts said. 'The Squirrels need a drink to get all the way to Mawson. I'll just fill up. Stay here.' He laughed again. 'Stay, stay here.'

Very funny, Stay thought as he got out of the helicopter. She could see him heading over to a pile of fuel drums half buried in the snow and after some fiddling around he dragged a fuel hose back over to the Squirrel. He pumped the fuel into the tank with a hand lever. When it was full, he pulled out the hose and took it over to the other helicopter. Stay could hear him laughing with Stretch and saw them looking over at her. When the refuelling was done, Nuts packed everything carefully away and clambered into the pilot seat again.

'Now let's get you looking your best,' he said. 'That's no way for a celebrity to travel.'

Nuts pulled Stay out of the mailbag and settled her properly on the front seat. He clipped the seatbelt across her chest and then positioned a pair of heavy earphones on her head. 'There you go, dude,' he said. 'An official V-I-D. Very Important Dog.'

He flicked the switches again and the rotors began to spin. Now that Stay could see everything it was much more exciting.

'Ready for liftoff?' Nuts looked over at her. 'Now we don't have an audience, we can really have some fun.'

You bet, Stay thought.

'Up, up and away!' Nuts said. This time they lifted up in such a fast takeoff that Stay had trouble keeping her eyes focused. In a matter of seconds they were in the sky and she was looking down on Antarctica.

It was majestic! Ice and snow stretched out as far as she could see, glistening in the sunshine.

'That's the Amery Ice Shelf,' Nuts said. 'Beautiful, eh? Now we follow it towards the sea and remember to turn left!'

They flew across ice and snow for what felt like a long time, until eventually Stay saw the ocean ahead. It was a deep blue, sparkling in the sunlight. A huge rock formation was coming up ahead of them: three big mountains rising out of the sea around a frozen bay.

Nuts dropped the helicopter into a steep dive to take them closer. 'That's Scullin Monolith. Biggest seabird breeding site in East Antarctica. Douglas Mawson landed there back in 1931 and claimed all this land for the British Empire. He was travelling by ship and I don't think he had dogs on that trip, but he was a great dog man. Used huskies on all his earlier exploration trips. Pity he ended up eating so many of them.'

He laughed and gave her a punch on the shoulder. 'Joke, Stay. No one will be eating you, don't worry. No one will have a chance to eat huskies either after this season. They're all going home. There'll be no more dogs in Antarctica.'

He pulled the helicopter up sharply and swung it into a swoop to the left. 'Can't go any closer than that. One of those special protected areas. I'm not allowed to go anywhere near nesting birds. I suppose I'd better get you to Mawson.'

He picked up the handheld radio microphone and put it up near his mouth. 'VJM-Mawson, this is Alpha-Foxtrot-Oscar.'

The radio crackled into life. 'Alpha-Foxtrot-Oscar, this is VJM-Mawson, reading you loud and clear.'

'Hi, dudes. Me and Sierra-Echo-Sierra are about twenty minutes away. I've got a local celebrity with me, so you'd best have a greeting party ready.'

Uh-oh, Stay thought. That didn't sound like she'd be kept a secret. She hoped nobody else would pinch her before she had a chance to get out to Chills.

'Looking forward to it. Thanks, Alpha-Foxtrot-Oscar. VJM-Mawson out.'

Nuts clicked the handset back into its holder and looked down at her. 'Well, girl, sorry, but the cat's out of the bag. Or should I say the dog's out of the mailbag?'

The pilot seemed to find his own jokes very funny. But Stay didn't mind. The sky was brilliant blue above them, the snow and the sea glistened below them, and, by the way Nuts was taking the joystick again, it looked as though he was going to show her some stunts before they landed.

Chapter 20

Stay could see a small group of people waiting at the helipad as Bluey and Stretch landed their helicopter first. Nuts lowered the second Squirrel slowly and smoothly to the ground, touching down with hardly a bump, as if he'd flown the whole trip in such a well-behaved way. He switched off the engine and the rotors slowed down and stopped spinning. He gave her a quick pat on the head.

'Glad you don't have a weak stomach, dude. Nice flying with you.'

He hopped out. Stay watched as people came over to greet Nuts, Bluey and Stretch, clapping them on the shoulders and shaking their hands. She saw someone point and then everyone came over to take a look at her.

Nuts opened Stay's door. 'This is Stay!' He took off her headphones, unclipped her seatbelt and lifted her out of the seat. People crowded around them as he turned and held her up high. There was a big cheer. Then Nuts turned to a woman standing towards the front.

'Stay, meet Jackie, leader of Mawson and first woman ever to lead an Antarctic base,' he said. 'Esteemed station leader, meet Stay of the Antarctic.'

'Well done!' Jackie smiled at Stay and patted Nuts on the back. 'We were sick of hearing about this dog from Davis Station and never getting to see her. How did you get her away from Dux?'

'Dude, I challenged him to a swimming competition. The person who stayed in the longest won. That was me, of course. So I told him I wanted the dog.'

That's not true! Stay thought indignantly.

'Actually, it wasn't me,' Nuts said when the noise died down. 'I'm not allowed to say who liberated Stay from Davis, but I'm entrusted to deliver her to Chills at Bechervaise Island. He's her rightful owner, apparently.'

'Chills?' Jackie said, and turned to look out over the bay.

Stay followed the woman's gaze and saw a rocky island offshore. It looked a long way across the sea ice. She remembered that it was covered in nesting penguins and she wondered how she'd get there. Not by helicopter anyway — Nuts wasn't allowed to fly near nesting birds.

'You've just missed him,' Jackie said. 'We brought him in for a shower and some food yesterday and dropped him back out on a quad bike. He's not due in again until Christmas.'

Stay felt a moment of alarm. She knew Christmas was close, but even a few days was a long time in Antarctica. Anything could happen in that time.

'Never mind,' the station leader said. 'We'll look after her till he gets in again. And besides, it will give her a chance to get acquainted with the huskies. They're dying to meet her, I'm sure.'

Nuts looked at his watch. 'Sounds good,' he said. 'We haven't got long. Is it too early to start the party?'

'Most people are still at work, but we can take a long lunch break today,' Jackie said. 'In the meantime, why don't we take Stay over to the husky line? Got your cameras, everyone?'

Stay felt a rush of excitement. Her first dogs since Jet! And they were Antarctic dogs. She couldn't wait to make some new friends.

Chapter 21

Nuts carried Stay high on his shoulder, followed closely by Jackie and about ten other people. Everyone was keen to witness her meeting with the huskies.

Stay was looking out eagerly to catch her first glimpse of the dogs. She heard them giving out a series of sharp barks and howls before she saw anything. There were a lot of them, by the sound of it!

Then they rounded the corner of one of Mawson's big rectangular buildings and there were the dogs, each chained to its own spot on two long lines. At the sight of Stay and all the humans, they jumped to their feet and started barking. *There are more than twenty*, Stay thought as she dizzily tried to count them, and she could see three pups near one of the females.

A large black husky, who was first in one of the lines, pulled against his collar and barked. *Who are you?*

'Quiet, dogs!' a man called out before Stay could answer. He stepped forwards and the huskies fell silent.

Nuts carried Stay over to the big black dog and put her down in front of him. 'Last huskies in Antarctica, meet the first Labrador in Antarctica,' Nuts said. 'In fact, Stay will be the very last dog in Antarctica if she doesn't go home on the ship with you. Stay, meet the Mawson huskies. This is Blackie, and that's Cocoa with the puppies. Back there are Morrie and Ursa and Cardiff and Nina and Pedro and ...'

Stay stopped listening to the dogs' names as Blackie lifted his lip and growled at her.

Cocoa, the brown female, sniffed and then sat down. *What are you? You look a bit like a dog, but you don't smell like one.*

I am a dog, Stay answered. *Well, sort of.* She realised that the only other real dog she'd met was Jet, and, being a Guide Dog, he had understood exactly what she was. Stay didn't know how to explain herself to the huskies.

She remembered she'd been able to talk to Jet just as if she was a living dog. *You can understand me, can't you?* she said to Blackie. *That proves I'm a dog.*

Blackie growled again and turned his back and for some reason this made all the people laugh.

Cocoa came closer and started sniffing Stay all over. *I don't believe you're a dog. You smell wrong.*

I'm a dog that helps blind people.

Oh? Cocoa sounded doubtful. *How do you help them?*

I raise money for them, Stay said.

The other dogs were barking, pulling at their tethers and straining to get close. *What's she saying? What kind of dog is she?*

Blackie started walking around Stay with stiff legs. *You're not an Antarctic dog, that's for sure. We are the huskies of the Antarctic!*

Only till the end of summer, Stay said, then wished she could bite the words back.

Blackie's answering growl was more like a snarl. *What do you mean?*

All the huskies are being taken out of Antarctica at the end of summer and never coming back, Stay said.

The dogs started barking furiously and the hair lifted on the back of Blackie's neck. *How do you know that?*

Stay wished she could roll on her back and show her belly to Blackie, the way that dogs told each other they were harmless and just wanted to be friends. *I heard the humans talking about it.*

There was silence and the dogs all stared. Blackie advanced on her, the fur on his hackles raised, and Stay wished that Nuts would pick her up. But the humans made no effort to rescue her.

No dog can understand humans talking, except for commands, Blackie snapped. *You're not a dog and, what's more, you're a liar!*

Blackie! Cocoa was wagging her tail just a little. *Give her a chance.*

No! Blackie barked so loudly that every dog on the line could hear him.

Stay stared at him, finding it hard to believe. How could this meeting have gone so wrong? She'd been so looking forward to becoming friends with some other dogs. How could she have known they didn't understand human speech like she did?

Blackie glared at the huskies. *You're all forbidden from talking to this thing. She's no dog, and she's to be ignored!*

At Blackie's order all the dogs started howling and throwing themselves against their chains. The racket was deafening and Stay again wished Nuts would pick her up and get her away. It was embarrassing. She'd rather be back at the Last Husky.

She could hear Nuts finally coming forwards, but before he could reach her, Blackie jumped up. Stay tensed, wondering if he was going to bite her, but he had something else in mind. Before Nuts could pick her up, Blackie lifted his leg and Stay felt a stream of liquid run over her back. It started out warm and then froze almost immediately.

The humans, even the ones who'd lost interest in watching and had started talking among themselves, all started to laugh. Stay wished she could just disappear into thin air, but nothing happened and no one rescued her. The dogs barked and barked, and the humans laughed and laughed. Only Cocoa looked at her, but Stay was too ashamed to meet the husky's eyes. Where was Chills when she needed him?

Chapter 22

Nuts was still giggling as he washed Stay from head to toe with a wet, soapy sponge in a bathroom off the Mawson LQ. Stay wished he'd stop. The whole incident was so embarrassing she just wanted to forget it. But she'd heard cameras snapping while Blackie was weeing on her, and she suspected everyone else would remember it for a long time.

'There you go, girl,' Nuts said, wiping her down with a fresh towel. 'Clean as a whistle.'

Stay had no idea why a whistle would be clean, and she didn't care. She willed Nuts to put her back into the mailbag and hide her somewhere till Chills could come and get her. She didn't want to see anyone at Mawson Station. She just wanted to disappear.

'OK, Stay, time for lunch,' Nuts said, hanging up the towel. 'Ready?'

No way, Stay thought, staring at him.

Nuts gave her a pat on the head. 'You know, you're not bad company, are you? Perhaps I should take you away again in the Squirrel. What do you reckon? Want to be a helicopter dog? See Antarctica from the air?'

It wasn't a bad idea, Stay had to admit. She'd liked riding in the passenger seat in the front of the Squirrel.

'You'll be even more famous now,' Nuts said. 'The dog who was weed on by the huskies. Ha ha!'

Stay changed her mind in an instant. Everywhere Nuts went, that story would follow, she realised. She'd be introduced as the dog who was weed on by huskies. It wasn't the kind of reputation she needed, not as a fundraiser for the Royal Guide Dogs. Anyway, Nuts was too fond of a joke for Stay's liking. She was sure Chills would never have let her be treated like that.

She concentrated on Nuts and willed him to leave her at Mawson. She just wanted to see Chills. He must have understood because he picked her up, tucked her under his arm and headed for the Mess without further comment.

Stay felt all her embarrassment return as they arrived in the Mess and everyone turned to face her. She cringed, waiting for them all to start laughing again. She looked down at the ground.

But a strange thing happened. Instead of laughter, Stay heard the sound of clapping. She couldn't believe her ears and looked up. What was going on?

Nuts carried her between the long tables and chairs, holding her high in the air, and people clapped as she went past. At the end of one of the tables she saw someone had set a special place with a dog bowl and a white napkin. Nuts put her down in the chair and tucked the napkin into Stay's collar so it hung in a smooth white triangle down her front.

Jackie, who was seated next to her, stood up and clanged her knife against her glass. Everyone quietened down.

'We have a special visitor with us,' she said in a loud voice. 'Stay the dog is our celebrity guest today. She's been through Neptune's welcome to sailors travelling below sixty degrees south and now she's had a unique welcome from the huskies too. That makes her a real Antarctican.'

Really? Stay thought. She started to feel a little less ashamed.

'Stay has had her Antarctic initiation, so I don't want any further shenanigans,' Jackie said. 'No silly tricks; no taking her to dangerous places for photographs. Understood?'

Everyone was nodding and smiling and when Jackie called them to they all raised their glasses in Stay's direction.

'A toast to Stay of the Antarctic, the newest resident of Mawson Station,' Jackie said.

'To Stay of the Antarctic!' everyone echoed, and drank.

'Now eat up!' Jackie said, and sat down. Everyone picked up their cutlery and began to eat. Stay saw that the food was also good on Mawson. Lunch was grilled fish, cauliflower cheese, peas, potatoes and salad. Over on the dessert bench there was ice-cream and something that smelt like blueberry crumble.

She looked around at the room. The faces were mostly unfamiliar, though she could see one or two people who'd come on the ship from Hobart and gone over to Mawson by Twin Otter, just as Chills and Beakie had. It would take her days to remember them all and really, she just wanted to go to Bechervaise Island, or Beche as most people called it. She wished she could will Chills to come over and get her, but the island was definitely too far away for her to reach his thoughts. She had to be looking at someone, or at least be very close to them, to be able to influence them as Jet had taught her.

She wondered if the huskies knew how to do that. It would be much harder for them, she supposed, as they couldn't understand human speech. The more she thought about it, the more she realised that dog life would be very confusing if you couldn't understand what humans were saying. If Chills had just picked her up in Hobart and bundled her into a bag, and she didn't know the meaning of the word 'Antarctica', she'd have had no idea where she was bound, or for how long.

Come to think of it, the huskies had spent their whole lives in Antarctica. Hobart would be as shocking for them as Antarctica had been for Stay.

The huskies! Stay felt a rush of shame just thinking of them. She so badly wanted to be friends with them, but Blackie had disliked her on first sight and made sure the rest of them wouldn't be friendly either. All because she was different. Didn't they understand she was still a dog? She felt like a dog, she looked like a dog, she could talk to other dogs. If she wasn't a dog, then what did they think she was?

It was a confusing line of thought and Stay was quite relieved when it was interrupted by the appearance of a tall man with wild hair and the longest, woolliest beard she'd ever seen. She couldn't help staring as he bent down to talk to Jackie.

'How's it going, Baldy?' she asked him.

'Cool, Boss Lady,' he said. 'Hey, I've been thinking about that dog.'

What about me? Stay thought.

'Windy and me are going out to Rumdoodle Hut tomorrow to give the huskies a run. We'll come back over the sea ice by Ring Rock. Be gone about three days, back in plenty of time for Christmas. We could swing by Beche on the way back and drop Stay off. There's still plenty of ice on that side, so we can get across with the sledge. Give Chills and Beakie a little surprise.'

Oh, yes! Stay thought. If she was off the station, then no one else could dognap her, hide her, chain her up to something, or wee on her. She'd be on her way to Chills.

'That's a very roundabout trip for dropping off the dog,' Jackie said, wrinkling her forehead. 'Anyway, Chills will be in for Christmas in a few days.'

Baldy grinned. 'It's a jolly. That's the point. There is no point.'

Jackie shrugged. 'Righteo then. Make sure the sea ice is safe before you cross. I don't want to be sending out a Search and Rescue.'

'Sure thing,' Baldy said. 'No "SAR" for us.'

Stay could see him grinning under his beard. He leant over and gave her a pat on the head.

'Looks like you're coming with us, Stay,' he said. 'Don't worry, I only look like a wild beast.'

Jackie laughed and then frowned. 'Don't take any risks to deliver a plastic dog, Baldy. No mischief.'

'We're in Antarctica,' Baldy said, his eyes wide and an innocent look on his face. 'What could possibly go wrong?'

'That's exactly what worries me,' Jackie said.

Baldy winked at her before he turned away and Stay wondered what Jackie was worried about. Baldy looked like a very trustworthy guy. A little too hairy for Stay's taste, but nice enough for all that.

It wasn't till he'd sat back down at his place and started eating again that she realised exactly what he meant.

A sledging trip with the huskies. The huskies who hated her. Oh, no.

Chapter 23

The preparations for their trip to Rumdoodle Hut were nearly done and a group of people from the station had come out to see them off. Despite her worries about the huskies, Stay was quite excited. This would be her first field trip in Antarctica. She wasn't going on a quad bike or in a Hägg but on a real dog sledge.

'There won't be too many more sledging trips in Antarctica,' Baldy said as he carried her to the sledge. 'This is a historic moment, Stay. One of the last chances to be like the old-time explorers.'

Windy waved at them. 'Can you lash her on?' he called. 'I'm just going to get the dogs.'

Baldy put Stay on top of the heavily loaded sledge and began tying her down. Like everyone else in Antarctica, he knew how to tie good, strong knots, and Stay felt him pull down hard on the ropes to make sure she was securely attached.

'Don't want you falling off,' Baldy said, giving her a pat on the back. 'OK, folks, she's ready for photos.'

Everyone who'd come to wave goodbye started taking pictures. Stay heard a bark and saw that Windy was bringing the first husky down. He held Cocoa by her harness, keeping her front feet in the air so she could only walk on her back legs. Stay watched, fascinated, as Windy took Cocoa to the front of the sledge and clipped her to the tow rope.

'There you go, girl,' he said, and patted her. 'Don't worry, your puppies will be fine on station.'

Meanwhile Baldy had gone to get the next dog and he returned with Blackie, holding him up in the air by the harness too. As each dog was secured, the team barked and snarled furiously. One dog managed to pull away from Windy and started a loud fight with another member of the team. Baldy and Windy had to pull the dogs apart and Stay was shocked. Guide Dogs never fought with each other, but it looked like a regular occurrence among the huskies.

Blackie was at the front and Stay hoped he might not see her. But as Baldy brought the last dog out, Blackie turned his head and saw Stay sitting up on the sledge.

He froze. His hackles rose and his upper lip lifted in a snarl. Stay was too far away to hear what he said, but she was sure it wasn't friendly. The other dogs turned their heads and stared at her, then all started barking.

'They don't like you much, do they?' Windy said. 'I guess they can't figure out if you're real.'

I am real, Stay thought indignantly.

But the dogs hadn't stopped barking and Stay could see Baldy was having trouble getting the last one harnessed. The huskies snapped at each other and turned in circles and he had to yell at them.

'Are you ready?' he called out to Windy. 'I have to get the huskies running.'

Windy gave Baldy the thumbs-up. 'Ready!'

'Righteo, folks,' Baldy called. 'One of the final Mawson sledging trips is now departing. Stand clear. Windy, get behind me!'

Everyone laughed then, though Stay couldn't understand why. She didn't have time to think about it, as Baldy yelled, 'Are you ready, dogs? Mush!' and let go of the harnesses. The huskies sprang forwards, barking. The sledge lurched and they were off, passing a blur of waving hands and faces. Windy ran alongside the sledge and jumped onto the back, standing on the runners just behind where Stay was lashed. Baldy kept running alongside the dogs, calling out commands and struggling to keep up with them.

Once the huskies were moving, they seemed to forget about Stay. They spread out in a fan shape in front of the sledge, running at a steady pace. She saw how much they loved their work, throwing themselves hard against the harnesses, pulling the sledge across the snow as if they could run forever. *They're just like the Guide Dogs*, she thought. Loyal and hard-working creatures. She wished they didn't dislike her so much. Couldn't they see they had lots in common with her?

After a while, Stay forgot about the huskies and started to notice the land around them. The wind rushing past her face was cold, but it was a clear sunny day and Stay could see for kilometres. They were heading inland, away from the station and up towards the plateau. She could see a big mountain range ahead of them. It looked quite close. Metal drums marked parts of their route so they could pass safely around the dangerous crevasses, which looked like big, dark blue cracks in the ice.

After the huskies had hauled the sledge for four hours, Stay realised that distances were deceptive in Antarctica. The faraway cliffs didn't look any closer than when they'd started out. Baldy and Windy had swapped places so now Baldy rode on the back and Windy ran beside the team, and they'd stopped for a few breaks to rest the dogs.

Eventually the steep cliffs rising out of the ice looked closer and then Stay saw a battered green box come into view on a rocky hillside ahead. Windy looked back and pointed.

Baldy waved to show he'd seen it. 'There's Rumdoodle!' he said to Stay. 'Best place for a jolly in the whole of Mawson.'

It wasn't long before they pulled up near the hut. It looked just like one of the shipping containers that the *Aurora Australis* had carried down full of cargo, except there were windows cut out of it and a door on one side, with a little porch. Stay saw it was bolted to the rocks beneath and held in place with heavy steel cables. She supposed that was to keep it anchored during a blizzard, and was pleased with herself for working it out. She was starting to get the hang of Antarctica.

Baldy unharnessed the dogs one at a time and ran them to a tether line near the hut. Each dog was secured to its own holding spot, out of reach of the other dogs. By the time he'd finished, Windy had unlashed the pack on the sledge that held the dogs' food, and in a matter of minutes he had a block of Antarctic dog food, called pemmican, in front of each dog. Neither Baldy nor Windy had stopped to eat or drink, Stay noticed. The dogs came first.

She was glad, for the dogs were so busy eating that they'd forgotten about her for a while. Windy lifted her down onto the snow, and she waited while they unpacked the sledge and carried boxes and bags inside. Although the sun didn't set, it was low on the horizon and the temperature had dropped. The breeze was picking up, and Stay could feel how cold it was getting. She wondered how the huskies kept warm.

At last the unloading was done and Baldy came around and picked her up. 'Coming in? Windy's got the heater going and dinner's on the way.'

That sounds great, Stay thought. She looked across at the huskies. Each one was curled up in the snow. They were all staring at her silently, except for Blackie.

He snarled in her direction. *A real dog, eh? No real dog goes inside. No real dog rides on the sledge. The real dogs are out here. We'll be waiting for you, tomorrow. Don't forget it.*

Stay's heart sank. Her chances of making friends with the huskies were more remote than ever.

Chapter 24

That night a blizzard blew in and the wind roared around the hut, making it rock. When Stay looked out the window, all she could see was white.

Baldy, Windy and Stay remained inside all the next day. The gas heater made it warm and cosy, and the men read books, played cards and Scrabble and cooked up delicious-smelling meals and mugs of hot chocolate on the tiny stove. They spent hours unpacking the stores they'd carried with them and restocking the food supplies of the hut for future visitors. Windy, who was bored with being stuck inside when he wanted to go exploring, rearranged the cans and packets of food and blocks of chocolate, making patterns.

'Check out this one!' he said, waving a block of chocolate in the air. 'The use-by date is nearly ten years ago!'

'That's nothing,' Baldy replied. 'We found a depot with old ANARE ration packs in it a few years back. The jam was over twenty years old. It was the station favourite for months.'

Windy opened the chocolate, broke off a row and stuffed it in his mouth. 'Tastes fantastic.'

'Chuck it over,' Baldy said.

Windy threw him the chocolate. 'I guess we'd better take all the pemmican back to the station,' he said sadly. 'Won't be any more dog trips out here.'

'Is it time for the sched yet?' Baldy asked.

'Yep. I'll get it started.'

Stay pricked up her ears. Morning and night they made a 'sched', a scheduled radio call back to the station to report they were all right and check on the weather. When Baldy switched on the radio, they sometimes heard other field parties making their scheds and chatting to each other as well as to Mawson Station's comms operator.

Stay listened to a lively conversation between Baldy and Windy and two other groups — one in the Prince Charles Mountains and another at Fang Peak field hut. She was starting to feel sleepy by the time the last radio sched came in. But she was suddenly wide awake when Chills's voice crackled over the radio.

'VJM-Mawson, this is VJM-3 sitrep.'

'Hi, VJM-3. Hearing you loud and clear. VJM-Mawson standing by.'

Baldy held his finger to his lips and nodded in Stay's direction. 'Don't mention Stay. Keep her a surprise,' he said to Windy.

The radio crackled and Stay strained to hear Chills's voice as he did his sched. 'We're still in the apple huts on Beche, surprise surprise,' he said. 'All fit and well. We'll be playing a few more rounds of rummy if this weather keeps up. Next time someone comes out, can you bring us a jar of Vegemite? Beakie's eaten the lot. Night, everyone. Out.'

'Thanks, VJM-3. VJM-Mawson out.' The radio went silent.

Windy peered out of a window into the whiteness. 'We've got to head back tomorrow,' he said. 'Not much of a jolly.'

'Are you kidding?' Baldy asked. 'One of the last sledging trips in Antarctica? Anyway, just getting off station is a jolly as far as I'm concerned.'

Windy started to make baked beans with melted cheese for dinner. A while after they'd finished eating and washing up, a loud blast ripped through the hut. Stay looked around to see where the noise had come from. Baldy jumped to his feet and started waving his book in front of him, while Windy kept reading calmly.

'Can't you go outside to fart?' Baldy asked, holding his hand over his nose.

Windy shrugged. 'Not in a blizzard, mate. You'll have to put up with it.'

Baldy shook his head in disgust. 'You must have been eating pemmican. You smell worse than a husky.'

'Be grateful you can run in front of me when we're sledging,' Windy said. 'There's no getting away from husky farts when they're pulling you on a sledge.'

Now I know where Windy's nickname came from, Stay thought. But she wondered how the huskies were managing. Surely anything out in the storm would freeze to death? Windy and Baldy took it in turns to go out and check on them and take out food and freshly melted snow for water, so they were obviously still alive, but Stay hadn't seen any shelter for them. She wondered how cold it would need to be before Windy brought the dogs inside to keep them warm.

By the second morning, the blizzard had blown itself out. When Baldy carried Stay outside into the sunshine, she looked around to see where the huskies were. Snow lay thickly all around the hut like a white blanket. She couldn't see a single one of them and started to panic.

Windy gave a whistle and suddenly there was a stir in the snow. A head broke through and there was a deep 'woof' that Stay recognised as Blackie's. He pushed up until his whole body appeared, his fur covered in white like talcum powder. He gave a huge shake, sending snow flying in all directions, and then barked.

All around him the snow moved as the rest of the huskies woke up, broke through the surface, stood up and shook.

'What do you think of that, Stay?' Windy asked. 'Tough little critters, aren't they? Just dig a hole in the snow and sleep through the blizzard. But they'll be desperate to get moving today after lying still all day yesterday. So we'd better get packed quick smart and leave for Beche. Christmas is coming and we don't want to get stuck out here in another blizzard and miss it.'

He put Stay down in the snow and went over to the sledge. It had frozen in place and he had to lean on it and rock back and forth to crack the runners free. Baldy started to check the dogs, rolling each over on its back to inspect its paws.

For a while Stay thought the huskies might have forgotten about her, but when Blackie had been inspected and patted by Baldy and was standing again, he looked over in her direction and growled. Many of the other dogs growled too, following his lead.

Stay decided to ignore the huskies. It seemed there was nothing she could do to make friends with them.

The sledge was going to Bechervaise Island and she'd be back with Chills. He was the human who most understood her. She could hardly wait.

'Right, let's get loaded,' Baldy called out to Windy. They both turned around and headed into the hut.

Stay watched them go inside and then heard another growl, much closer this time. It sounded like Blackie. She glanced backwards and saw that he must have slipped out of his collar. He walked up to her, his legs stiff and his head low, the way the huskies walked when they were about to start a fight. Stay tensed, hoping he wouldn't wee on her again. It had been embarrassing enough the last time.

Blackie bared his teeth. *Had a nice time inside the hut? All warm and cosy?*

Yes, Stay gulped. She didn't know what else to say.

You know nothing about Antarctica. He circled her. The fur on his neck was standing up and Stay wanted to shrink away from him. *You can't even stay outside in a blizzard. So don't call yourself a dog!*

Stay said nothing. Blackie kept circling. *You think you've got those people just where you want them, carrying you around, keeping you inside, taking photos, putting you on the sledge. Well, they can't protect you all the time.*

Stay shivered. Blackie's growls were scary and it was a horrible thought that he was waiting to get her. She'd seen how viciously the dogs fought each other even though they were on the same team — and she couldn't fight back. She was relieved when Baldy appeared at the door, loaded down with bags, and started walking towards the sledge. Blackie scampered away and stood at his place on the tether line so no one could see he'd been near Stay.

Baldy and Windy went in and out of the hut with the baggage and stacked it on the sledge. Windy tied it down, working quickly to knot the ropes and pull down on them hard so everything was securely fastened.

Baldy headed off for a last trip to the toilet and Windy picked Stay up and put her on top of the baggage. He looped a rope around her legs, pulled it down tight and knotted it so she was held in place. Then he stood up straight. 'Now where's my camera?' he murmured, patting his pockets. 'Must be inside still. Got to get a shot of you at the hut, Stay.' He headed back into the hut.

As soon as Windy disappeared, Blackie ran back to the sledge. He stuck his snout near Stay's leg, sank his teeth into the rope holding her in place and started gnawing it. He braced himself in the snow and shook his head back and forth, growling. His teeth must have been very sharp, for Stay could feel the rope giving way beneath his attack. She sent a frantic thought in Windy's direction for him to come out quickly.

The door of the toilet creaked open and Baldy stepped out. He was carrying a black plastic bag that was tied shut. 'Are we ready to go yet?' he called.

Blackie let go of the rope. Stay could feel that he'd damaged it badly, but it was still holding. He ran back around to the other dogs and stood in his usual place, his tail wagging and his tongue hanging out as if nothing was wrong.

Windy came out of the hut, clutching his camera. 'We're ready!' He shoved the door firmly shut and stomped across the snow to the sledge. 'Smile, Stay!' he called, and took her photo, lining it up to get the hut in the background. He shoved the camera in his pocket and went across to the tether line. 'How did you get out of your collar?' he asked Blackie, grabbing the harness. 'Bad dog.' He walked him to the front of the sledge and attached him, then went back for the next dog.

Baldy came over to the sledge with the plastic bag. 'Now where will I put this?' he mused.

Check my rope! Stay thought.

Baldy opened a box and put the bag inside, being very careful. Stay couldn't get his attention, no matter how furiously she sent him her thoughts.

'Poo bag packed?' Windy said, looking up from the dogs.

Baldy made a face. 'Can't believe we have to carry it back to the station.'

'It's the new environmental protocol,' Windy said. 'A lot of things are going to change around here. Soon the satellite system will be working and then you'll be able to just pick up the phone and call home. Nothing will be the same. And no huskies.'

'Have you picked up the huskies' poo?'

Windy shrugged. 'We don't have to take theirs back. There'll be no fresh dog poo on Antarctica after the end of summer.'

Please look at my rope! Stay thought again, trying Windy this time.

'At least Stay doesn't poo,' Baldy said. 'Best thing about her. Are we ready to go? Everything lashed tight?'

'All good,' Windy said. 'Let's go.'

He came around to the back of the sledge, released the brake and called, 'Mush!'

There was a lurch as the sledge moved forwards. Stay wobbled a little, but the rope held her in place. Blackie hadn't had time to gnaw right through it, she realised. Windy jumped on the back of the sledge right behind her. If the rope did snap, he'd catch her. It only had to hold her for as long as it took to get to Bechervaise Island, and to Chills.

Chapter 25

It was a beautiful day for sledging. The sun sparkled on the snow, the sky was a deep blue and there was hardly any wind. The dogs, full of energy after a day of sleeping in the snow, pulled so hard that the sledge flew along. Windy rode on the back while Baldy ran alongside. Every hour or so they'd change places.

Stay had watched Windy and Baldy trace their sledging route on the map the night before. They were making a wide arc back towards the coast that would bring them out on the sea ice west of the station. They'd make a detour across the ice to Bechervaise Island to drop Stay off, and head back to the station afterwards.

Stay was anxious about falling off at first, but she soon realised that the rope holding her in place was still working. She relaxed and began to enjoy the sights.

After a few hours, they came down off the plateau and onto the sea ice. It took a while for them to find a safe crossing, for the area of ice at the shoreline, the tide crack, was badly buckled and cracked due to the tide movements under the frozen surface.

But eventually they found a way across and then it was easier going for the huskies on the ice, as the sledge slid along freely and the surface was smoother. They passed a group of Weddell seals, looking like enormous slugs, asleep on the ice near an open hole. The adult seals lazily opened an eye to watch them pass, yawned and fell back asleep again. The young seal pups were more curious, lifting their heads to watch the huskies with wide, dark eyes, and then scratching themselves with the claws at the end of their flippers. Their mouths turned up in permanent smiles that made Stay want to smile back at them.

'Hey, look at that!' Windy yelled, right in her ear. Baldy turned his head and Windy pointed. Stay could see a big dark shape lying on the ice further out. Baldy shouted a command and the dogs turned slightly so the sledge was heading towards the shape. As they came closer, Stay peered to see what it was.

'A leopard seal!' Windy yelled again, nearly deafening Stay. Baldy waved a hand to show that he'd heard.

Unlike the Weddell seals, the leopard seal had a big, square-shaped head and its shiny coat was mottled and spotty. As they approached, Baldy ran forwards and grabbed Blackie's harness to bring him to a halt, while Windy put on the drag brake, leaning hard on its pole so it scraped along the ice.

The dogs barked furiously and the leopard seal lifted up its head and roared back at them. Stay saw that its huge mouth was full of teeth. It looked dangerous and she wished Baldy would take them away.

'Don't worry, Stay,' Windy said in her ear. 'It can't move fast on land. But watch out if you ever see one in the water. Don't go near the edge!'

Baldy turned Blackie slightly and called out, 'Mush!' and Windy let the brake off. The dogs began running again, away from the seal, though Stay could feel they wanted to go closer and give it a nip. They were brave, that was for sure.

A single penguin, standing alone on the ice, saw them coming and ran towards them, his flippers spread wide as if he wanted to come with them. *Maybe he's taken a wrong turn and forgotten the way to the sea*, Stay thought. She hoped he knew to keep away from the leopard seal. He looked just the right size to make a good dinner.

They stopped for a break. Windy gave the black dogs a snow bath to help them cool down after their run. The men drank hot chocolate out of a Thermos and ate biscuits. The dogs chewed on blocks of pemmican and

Stay wished she could eat. *Food looks like so much fun*, she thought.

A breeze blew across Stay's back and she looked over to the horizon. A line of thin white clouds was forming and for the first time she could remember, the breeze felt warm.

Baldy looked over in the same direction. 'There's no bad weather forecast today, is there?'

Windy shook his head. 'The Met Fairies said it would be sunny today and then a change would blow in tomorrow.'

'I don't like the look of that cloud.'

Windy laughed. 'That tiny thing? Don't be a wuss.'

'It's getting warm. That's a bad sign. Let's get going. Sea ice can break up any time.'

It seemed hard to imagine that a small, thin cloud could cause them any trouble, but both men stood and started packing up their lunch things and within minutes they were sledging again.

Baldy was right behind Stay and she could feel him turning his head to look in the direction of the cloud. It was growing thicker, Stay saw, and the air felt even more strangely warm.

Baldy called to Windy and pointed. Stay followed the line of his finger. Ahead of them she could see a scatter of rocky islands in the sea ice. They looked familiar and she realised one of them was Bechervaise! It wasn't far now, just a few kilometres until she saw Chills at last.

But clouds were building up fast and Stay saw that a blizzard was blowing in across the sea ice towards them, just the way squalls had blown in across the water when she was on board the *Aurora Australis*. She remembered what Kaboom always said — that Antarctic weather was the most unpredictable in the world and, no matter what the forecast, anything could happen.

Baldy jumped off the back of the sledge and started running alongside the dogs with Windy — so his weight wasn't making them slower, Stay supposed. She looked at how fast the clouds were moving. It would be a near thing to make the island before they found themselves in the blizzard.

'Hey!' she heard Baldy call out to Windy. 'I don't like the look of this. I think we should get off the ice and head for the station!'

Windy looked over at the approaching line of white snow. 'That's coming up fast! Good idea, I reckon.'

Windy yelled, 'Leeeeeft!' and Blackie changed direction, with the rest of the dogs following. The sledge went around in a big curve till they were heading for the station, with the squall almost behind them. The dogs sped up and Stay knew they sensed the danger too.

Though she was terribly disappointed they weren't going to the island, Stay could see the blizzard was nearly on them. They'd be lucky to make it back to the station without getting caught. She'd heard expeditioners talking about 'whiteouts' when they couldn't see anything in front of them, not even a hand held up to their eyes, but so far she'd never been in one. It looked like she was about to experience it.

They bounced across the tide crack and started up a snow-covered slope. Windy, Baldy and the dogs were running hard and Stay saw Mawson Station's Redshed building appear over a hill. It looked small, but at least they were in sight of the station. She felt a wave of relief. Surely they were safe? They couldn't get lost that close.

Suddenly she felt a slam of icy wind on her back, so hard it felt like someone had hit her. The rope that Blackie had chewed jerked, and Stay rocked. The blizzard had caught them.

White snow streamed past and Stay could hardly see the dogs pulling the sledge. Baldy and Windy were two dark, blurry shapes on either side of the dog team. The men called out commands and the dogs slowed. They had to get back to the station as quickly as possible, but they couldn't run so fast, blinded by the blizzard.

Stay tried to sense how far away the station was, but she couldn't feel a thing through the flying snow. *All they have to do is keep going straight*, she thought. The sledge was moving freely across the snow, it wasn't far now.

Stay felt another jerk and the sledge bumped hard beneath her. It lurched and rocked to one side and she began to slip. The rope holding her on the sledge felt horribly loose.

She tried to send a thought to Windy or Baldy, but the snow was blowing so hard that she could barely see them. The sledge lurched again and tipped further, but somehow stayed upright.

Then Stay heard a loud crack. The snow under the sledge was giving way and there seemed to be nothing underneath it. They were over a crevasse! It must have been hidden by a snow bridge, but the weight of the sledge had broken through the snow and now she was looking straight down into a big blue crack in the ice that looked bottomless.

Faintly, through the blizzard, she heard Windy calling on the dogs to pull harder. The sledge twisted, then hit the ice on the edge of the crevasse and bounced. The rope holding Stay snapped under the strain.

She sent a despairing thought towards anyone who could hear.

HELP!

The sledge jerked and pulled ahead, out of the crevasse, but Stay wasn't on it. The last thing she saw was the sledge disappearing into the whiteout before she fell backwards, down-down-down into the deep crack in the ice.

Chapter 26

Stay scraped, bounced, dropped, clattered, almost stuck and fell again. The coins inside her rolled around and clanged from side to side. Finally she slammed down into a narrow part of the crevasse and felt herself wedge hard into the ice.

The echo of her fall seemed to go on and on and the coins spun inside her, eventually coming to a stop. Stay felt a pang of despair. If the tumble under the weight of Wreck had broken her leg, then this fall would surely crush her. She wasn't built for this kind of rough treatment.

As the echoes died away, Stay's sight adjusted. She was a long way down in the ice crevasse. It would be hard to get out. It looked like there was barely room for a person in the crevasse, and how would they get down to reach her anyway?

She was stuck lying on her back, looking up the

crevasse. She'd seen the beautiful blue cracks in icebergs while she was on the ship, but she'd never thought about being in one. Even in the gloom of the blizzard, the ice near the surface seemed to glow bright blue. It was like the neon light that Stay remembered from a shop window in Hobart.

Hobart felt a million kilometres away at that moment.

Stay wondered what was taking the men so long to turn around. Perhaps it was hard to stop the dogs so close to home. The longer they stayed out in the blizzard the colder they would get, and she knew the huskies would have one more reason to hate her.

I'm down here, Stay thought in the direction of Windy and Baldy.

She couldn't hear anything in return. She was wedged tight as a cork in a bottle. It was very cold and she could hear water dripping somewhere underneath her.

Baldy and Windy must have decided to go back to the station without her, Stay realised. It sounded like a dangerous blizzard up there, howling across the snow like a pack of wild dogs. It was true, being fibreglass, she couldn't freeze to death. It would be safer for everyone if they waited until the blizzard had passed before rescuing her.

The wind whistled over the top of the crevasse, making a noise like the one the people in the Last Husky made when they blew across the mouth of an empty bottle. It was a lonely sound.

Chapter 27

Stay didn't know how many hours passed before the wind dropped and everything went quiet.

She looked up. She could see the sides of the crevasse glowing blue above her, though she'd fallen so far into it that it was almost dark where she was. Above, at the surface, she saw that the blizzard had blown snow over the top of the icy crack and the snow had frozen into a bridge, covering the opening of the crevasse again.

That was why the men and the dogs hadn't seen the crevasse in the first place. It had been completely covered, invisible from the surface. They hadn't known it was there until the sledge had broken through it.

It was invisible again, and that would make it difficult for them to find her. She wondered how long it would take. She wasn't very far from the station — perhaps they wouldn't even need the dog sledge again.

Baldy and Windy could just get into their cold-weather clothing and use a couple of quad bikes to come looking.

They'd probably want a big breakfast before heading out into the cold, and it might take them an hour or two to get ready. It might be as late as lunch time before she was rescued. She'd hear them walking around and send them a strong thought about where she was. Easy.

Chapter 28

It was the time of year when the sun didn't set, so Stay had no way of knowing how much time had passed, except by how bored she was.

She was so bored she wanted to explode!

She'd remembered every adventure she'd had in Antarctica so far. She'd remembered every funny nickname and why it was given. She tried to remember every single person at Davis Station and everyone at Mawson Station. She even remembered all of the crew on the *Aurora Australis*. She remembered all the different meals the chefs had cooked up. She remembered the puppies and how cute they looked. It wouldn't be long until they grew up into big bad sledging huskies.

She remembered all the hiding places she'd been in. This one was the best. It would be very hard for someone who didn't know she was there to find her.

Very, very hard.

Nearly impossible.

Chapter 29

For the umpteen millionth time Stay strained her senses, trying to feel if any humans were nearby, but all she heard was silence. Silence so quiet that her ears rang. Silence so quiet that it felt loud.

As far as Stay could figure out, several days must have passed. *At least four,* she thought, *and perhaps five or even six.*

It had taken all that time for her to realise that no one was coming to look for her.

Windy and Baldy knew she'd been on the sledge when the blizzard struck, and they must have known she'd fallen off. Perhaps they hadn't known straight away — perhaps not until they got back to the station. But it shouldn't have taken long to mount an SAR — a Search and Rescue — just as Jackie had said she would if they got into trouble.

Stay already knew the huskies didn't like her.

Blackie had chewed on the rope so it would break. He wanted her to fall off. They were probably happy that she was lost. But she had believed the humans would look for her. They were the ones who'd brought her to Antarctica. Surely they wouldn't just forget about her?

It had taken days for her to understand that she was wrong. They didn't care.

Stay had been left alone before. When Chills and Beakie had hidden her in the Hägg and left her there for days after taking her money, she'd been furious with them. But they were just smuggling her ashore, and the money was perfectly safe. It all turned out fine.

This time Stay couldn't see any way it would turn out fine. She was stuck deep in a crevasse, hidden by a layer of snow, too far away to reach anyone with her thoughts.

As she lay there, Stay felt a terrible pain in her chest. She realised it was what people meant when they talked about being heartbroken. She wasn't sure if she had an actual heart, but the pain in the place where her heart would have been was real. The thought that none of those people cared for her was breaking her heart.

Where are you, Chills? she thought, but just softly. It was useless to project her thoughts.

She couldn't feel angry at Chills. He might have forgotten all about her, but she knew she would never forget him. She was a Labrador after all. She'd stay loyal to him right to the end.

With nothing else to do, Stay listened to the sounds that broke the Antarctic silence. It was so quiet that when faint sounds did come, she heard them with new clarity. She heard the harsh cries of big brown skuas and the shrill chattering of little white snow petrels, above her on the surface. Once she heard the trumpeting of an emperor penguin and another time the raucous calls of Adélies racing past on their way to the rookery, their feet making little crunching sounds in the snow. She sent a thought in their direction, but they didn't hear her.

The ice made noises as if it was alive: sharp cracks and creaks, groans and squeaks. The ice flowed like a river, Stay remembered. She'd heard a glaciologist telling a carpenter about it one night at the Last Husky. It was always moving, shifting, melting and reforming, flowing down towards the sea. Eventually it would break off in sections that would become icebergs.

Stay could hear the sound of dripping water as the Antarctic snow melted and collected in the bottom of the crevasse. It trickled away somewhere. To the sea, Stay supposed, underneath the layer of sea ice, which would also be melting now that summer was well advanced. She remembered that they'd turned around

160

just near the edge of the sea ice, so she wasn't far from the shore. If she strained her ears, she could hear the sea, washing back and forth.

When she concentrated hard, she heard very strange sounds from that direction: whistles and chirps that sounded like some machine Laser would have used to measure something. As she strained to hear them, she realised it was the Weddell seals talking to each other. The same seals she'd seen sleeping on the ice like great big slugs had a busy and graceful life under the water, singing as they swam about. She could understand a little of what they were saying — mostly about fish and finding mates — and she listened for a long time, wishing she could talk back to them.

She didn't know what she'd say to them, though. She was a fibreglass dog whose job was to raise money for the Royal Guide Dogs so they could help blind people. She'd been dognapped and carried to Antarctica, and she was staying for the summer to raise some more money. But she was stuck in the bottom of a crevasse, buried under a snow bridge, somewhere near Mawson Station. By the look of it, she would be there forever.

She didn't think that would be easy to explain to a seal.

Then she remembered the story that the glaciologist had told about Robert Falcon Scott and his men, who died on the way back from the South Pole. Their bodies had been left in the ice, which was slowly moving. One day they would be carried to the sea by the movement of the glacier.

The same thing would happen to her! One day, after many years, she'd come to the end of the glacier and the ice she was in would break off. She'd find herself in an iceberg floating on the ocean, and when the iceberg eventually melted, she'd fill up with water and sink. And there she would end her days, lying forever on the ocean floor.

She wouldn't be alone: there'd be seals and fish and krill and penguins and whales and all the other creatures that swam in Antarctica's oceans. But no people and no dogs.

There was nothing she could do about it. *My name's perfect*, Stay thought sadly. The only thing she could do was stay put, and remember Chills.

Chapter 30

Stay?

Stay had been dreaming of lying by the fire with Jet, back in Hobart, watching the flickering flames. There were puppies there with them, cute gold and black Labradors playing together. Stay was so full of money for the Guide Dogs that she couldn't move. She knew she had raised enough money for all of those puppies to be trained. Carol was sitting in the armchair by the fire, looking at her proudly. It was the best dream she'd had since falling into the crevasse.

She blinked sleepily. Everything was exactly the same. The light was still blue, the water was still dripping down underneath her, and the top of the crevasse was still covered with snow. The ice creaked loudly and she wondered if that was the sound that had woken her.

Are you there, Stay?

Stay would have jumped to attention if she could move. Plenty of times since falling into the crevasse she'd thought she heard something, but this time it sounded real.

Hello? She sent a thought back as hard as she could.

She's down there! I heard her.

Stay realised it was Cocoa whining. They were looking for her, at last! She was so relieved she wanted to cry. Up above she heard a bark then the sound of paws scratching in the snow. They'd brought the dogs to search for her. It wouldn't be long now till she was out of the crevasse.

Be quiet! Blackie growled at Cocoa. He still sounded angry.

Cocoa whined again. *But, Blackie, she's down there in the crevasse. We can't just leave her there.*

Of course we can. She's just a piece of plastic. I don't know why the humans care about her.

I am not plastic! I'm fibreglass! Stay thought.

She's an impostor, Blackie snapped. *If anyone barks and lets the humans know she's nearby, I'll bite them.*

Stay gave a silent whimper. She could hear the distant sound of human voices, but every single dog was quiet. Stay tried sending a thought towards the humans, but she was buried too far down to reach them. They'd never find her without help from the dogs, she realised.

Stay sent her thoughts towards the dogs. *Blackie, I have something to tell you.*

He didn't answer, but she could feel all the dogs listening.

It's about what will happen to you all when the humans take you out of Antarctica.

What? Cocoa asked, and Stay heard Blackie snap at her.

You're going on an adventure, like the one I've been on, Stay told them. *Firstly you'll go on the big orange ship across the sea to Hobart. When you get there, the dogs that have worked for a long time will go to new homes where they can rest. The other dogs are going across the world to a place called Minnesota in America. You'll be working over there, pulling sledges in the snow.*

What about my puppies? Cocoa asked.

They're going to America with you. You'll all be together.

How do you know this? Underneath his snarl, Blackie sounded scared.

I can talk to the humans. Chills especially. I heard them talking about it one night at the Last Husky. They're all very sad about you going. They wish you could stay. They're going to miss you.

There was a long silence, and then Blackie growled. *If you can really talk to Chills, then show us. He's up here with us, looking for you. None of the humans can see where you are, there's too much snow covering the crevasse. If you're so clever, then prove it.*

Chapter 31

CHILLS! I'M DOWN HERE! HELP!

Stay panted. She'd called and called Chills in her mind, but he was just too far away to hear her. She could barely hear the sound of distant footsteps any more. The humans and the dogs were moving further away from the crevasse. She'd thought being forgotten was terrible, but being left behind so close to rescue was even worse.

She thought of the Guide Dogs. They would never leave anyone in trouble. It wasn't something Labradors did. Right from the time they were puppies, they just wanted to help. She wondered if the husky puppies were the same. Huskies were also hard-working dogs that wanted to help humans. They weren't very different, really.

The sounds of the dogs had almost disappeared, and Stay felt a sob rising in her chest. She sent a final sad thought to Cocoa: *Look after your puppies. They're off on a great adventure.*

There was a long pause and then Stay heard a distant volley of barking. Cocoa was defying Blackie! She was leading the searchers to the crevasse.

The barking became louder and Stay could hear footsteps and human voices. Soon they were very close by and she could hear Cocoa sniffing and barking. There was a crunch in the snow above the crevasse and she saw that someone had poked a cane through. A gleam of daylight came in and then all the dogs were barking with excitement. All except Blackie, Stay noticed.

A torch flashed down the tide crack, blinding her, and a voice called down. 'Are you there, Stay?'

It was Chills! He hadn't abandoned her after all. Stay felt the pain in her chest disappear. She sent him the hardest thought of her life: *I'M HERE!*

'I can see her!' Chills yelled. 'She's at the bottom of the crevasse!'

Stay was weak with relief. He'd found her. She heard the sound of him roping up and within minutes he was abseiling down into the crevasse, the metal spikes on his boots scraping against the blue ice walls.

'Are you all right, Stay?' he asked, dangling in his abseiling harness just above her. 'You're well and truly slotted!'

Chills had grown such a huge beard since she last saw him that Stay hardly recognised him. *Just get me out*, she thought faintly.

It wasn't easy. Chills had to manoeuvre himself down as close as he could get to Stay and tie a rope around her. She was so tightly wedged in the crevasse that the rescuers above had to all pull on the rope. At last she came free with a huge jerk and a scrape that she felt through her whole body. They pulled her up through the ice and she banged from side to side, sending her coins rattling. At last, with Chills next to her, she reached the top.

'You're out!' he said, clambering over the lip of the crevasse and getting to his feet. 'Thank goodness. That's the best Christmas present ever.'

After the dark and cold of the crevasse, the sun felt deliciously warm. The light was so blinding that Stay couldn't make out who had come to help rescue her, though she could see at least six people and the same number of dogs. But there was no mistaking the applause that rose up.

'Three cheers for Stay!' That was the station leader, Jackie.

'Hip hip hooray!' everyone called.

'Are you hurt, Stay?' Chills asked, running his hands over her.

Stay felt scraped all over, but to her amazement it seemed she had no major damage from the fall. Even her wooden leg was still firmly in place.

'Just bumps and bruises, old girl. You'll be fine,' Chills said.

Say something to the huskies, Stay thought.

Chills bent down and hugged Cocoa. 'We'd never have found her without the dogs. Extra rations all round!'

When Stay sent the thought of extra blocks of pemmican to the huskies, they barked and jumped in the air in delight. *Perhaps they won't hate me so much any more*, she thought.

Chills hoisted Stay onto his shoulders. 'Let's get back to the station. And then I'm taking Stay out to Beche, where she'll be safe for the rest of the season! I'm not leaving her with anyone else! Ever!'

'Hurry up, folks,' Jackie said. 'Christmas dinner is starting any minute, and the chef will kill us if we let it get cold.'

Stay looked back over Chills's shoulder as they set off towards Mawson. Windy was leading Blackie. Unlike the other dogs, Blackie hadn't reacted to the news of extra rations. He was staring at Stay and he still looked angry.

She didn't care. She was with Chills at last, and they were going to Bechervaise. She'd be safe there.

Chapter 32

The whole station gathered for Christmas dinner
and the Mess was decorated with streamers and white
tablecloths. The chef and his helpers brought out the
food and laid it on the tables. Stay was amazed to see
they'd created a Santa's sleigh for each table, pulled by
big orange lobsters and stuffed with prawns. She could
smell other wonderful food on the way — roast chicken,
mashed potatoes, gravy and plum pudding with custard.

All the expeditioners looked eager to start eating,
but as they sat down there was a shout and everyone
pointed to the window. Santa was coming across the
snow, sitting in the back of a sledge being dragged by
the huskies. He pulled up outside and came into the
Mess, his face almost completely covered with a big
white beard.

He gave everyone a little package. There was even
one for Stay, which Chills opened. It was her own black

bow tie with pink spots, and everyone clapped when Chills put it on her.

'I missed you!' he whispered as he tightened it around her neck. 'I'm so glad we found you, Stay.'

I'm so glad too, Stay thought.

'You'll love it out at Beche with the penguins. They're really funny. Beakie and I have been having a great time. It will be even better with you there.'

Beakie was grinning at Stay from across the table. 'Lucky my feelings aren't hurt that Chills needs a Guide Dog for company.'

Everyone laughed, but Stay didn't mind. 'We were so worried about you,' Chills said. 'When I got here for the Christmas feast, they told me you were missing. People had been out searching for you, but no one could find you. I forced everyone to come out looking again. I wasn't going to leave you out there. No way.'

I'm glad, Stay thought.

'It's funny, but even Kaboom knew there was something wrong all the way over at Davis,' Chills said. 'She sent me a telex that said she'd been worried about you for days. She was sure something bad had happened.'

Stay thought of Kaboom and felt warm. Surely the Met Fairy hadn't heard Stay's thoughts all the way from Davis? It wasn't possible. But she must have felt something. Stay hoped she'd see Kaboom again sometime soon.

She felt a big hand on her head. Baldy and Windy had come over to pat her.

'Sorry about losing you out there, Stay,' Baldy said. 'Windy and I spent hours looking for you when the blizzard cleared, but the sledge tracks were covered. We didn't know you'd fallen in a crevasse.'

That's OK, Stay thought.

'We felt pretty bad, Stay,' Windy said. 'We're losing the dogs in Antarctica. We didn't want to lose you too. Sorry, old girl.'

Perhaps it was the Christmas spirit, but as she looked around the Mess at the smiling faces, Stay felt a funny feeling in her chest. It was a bit like the feeling she'd had in the crevasse when she thought her heart was breaking, but it was a happy feeling. The Antarctic humans felt like her family. She felt like she was home.

Chapter 33

Two months later

The Adélie penguin chick hopped over the rock and landed in front of Stay. Its brown fluff was starting to disappear and patches of smooth black and white feathers were showing through underneath. It looked ragged and messy as it waddled towards her, its flippers outstretched.

Hello, Stay thought.

The young penguin didn't answer. Stay was never sure if the birds could hear her thoughts or not. The Adélies would just stare at her when she tried talking to them. Their white-rimmed eyes meant they always looked surprised, so she couldn't tell what they were thinking.

The chick waddled right up to Stay and cuddled up close between her paws, out of the wind. Stay tried to keep her thoughts quiet in case she scared it off. The penguins were used to her now, but she'd never had one cuddle up before. It was almost as cute as a puppy.

The Adélie penguins were funny little clowns. The parents had still been sitting on their tiny chicks, keeping them warm, when Stay first arrived, but the little ones seemed to grow every day. Soon they were as big as the adults and they spent their time chasing them around, crying out for food. Before long the black-and-white parents spent most of their time fishing in the ocean and the rookery was full of big fluffy brown chicks. The neat nests of pebbles were scattered and messy, and bits of fluff lay around everywhere. Now the chicks were almost grown up. Soon they'd be heading out to sea to learn to fish for themselves.

Stay hadn't liked the strong, sharp smell of bird droppings when she first arrived, but she'd quickly got used to it and hardly even noticed the smell any more.

The sea ice in Horseshoe Bay had broken up just after Stay, Chills and Beakie had come out to Bechervaise Island after Christmas. The inflatable Zodiac boats couldn't travel when there was too much broken ice floating around, so they were marooned on the island for weeks. Stay hadn't minded at all. She'd had no responsibilities out there and no worries either. She'd been able to watch and listen to all the birds and animals, and enjoy the company of Chills and Beakie.

The men were working hard on their penguin research and Stay went out with them every day. She spent hours sitting on the rocks watching the Adélies while Chills and Beakie counted them, collected their poo and looked at it under microscopes, and stuck radio transmitters on the penguins' backs so they could track where they went.

Every night they went into the main apple hut, which was small and round and red, and cooked dinner on the gas stove. At bedtime, Chills carried her over to the second apple hut, which was even smaller, and put her right next to his bed. He often had long conversations with her before he went to sleep, talking about life in Antarctica and the things he'd done that day.

'You're a great listener, Stay,' he told her.

Stay wished she could stay there forever, watching the penguins and the seabirds and the seals and listening to Chills.

Perhaps this chick can feel the change of season coming, she thought, looking down at where it was huddled between her forelegs. The wind was very chilly, blowing with the promise of winter, and the ocean surface was looking greasy, which Chills said meant it was starting to freeze over again. It was late February, and the days were getting shorter. Summer was over.

'Hey, look at this, Beakie!' Chills had turned around from where he was picking up penguin poo and was looking at the chick sitting between Stay's legs.

Beakie turned around to look and gave a big grin. 'Sweet!'

Chills fished out his camera from his bag and took a picture. 'A nice finish to the season,' he said. 'I'm going to miss it out here. I don't want to go back to Australia.'

'I do,' Beakie said. 'I'm sick of the cold. I want to see trees and grass and people again.'

'I bet you'll be begging to come down again next season,' Chills said. 'That's what always happens. People can't wait to get home, and then they can't wait to get back here.'

Beakie shrugged. 'Maybe. I'd like it better on station, I reckon. It gets a bit lonely out here.'

But you've got us, Stay thought.

'What do you mean?' Chills said. 'You've got me and Stay! What more could you want?'

Beakie grinned. 'I wouldn't mind some female company. No offence, Stay, but I'd like some more women around the place.'

'There are more women coming down every year,' Chills said. 'Maybe you can find a woman doing penguin research next time.'

'We'll see,' Beakie said. 'It would be fun to hang out with those girls we came down with. What were their names again?'

Chills laughed. 'Don't pretend you've forgotten Kaboom and Laser. You don't fool me.'

Beakie looked shy. 'They were nice. It will be good to see them on the ship.'

Stay agreed. She liked the women too and was keen to see them again.

'Not Kaboom,' Chills said. 'Weather observers stay down all winter. She won't be coming back with us. Hopefully we'll get to see her at Davis when the ship calls through. I'd like to say goodbye.'

He sounds really sad, Stay thought. She knew how he felt. After Chills, Kaboom was her favourite person in Antarctica. Most people who'd come down on the *Aurora Australis* at the start of the season would be going home again, but a small number stayed down all winter to carry out more research and to keep the stations running. Kaboom was one of them. *If only she was coming home with us*, Stay thought.

Beakie shivered. 'Brrrr. No way I'd stay for winter. Too cold. And no sun for six weeks! I'd hate being in the dark that long.'

'Some people really love it,' Chills said. 'They get to see the southern lights. They're meant to be amazing.'

Beakie stroked his beard, which was nearly as long as Chills's. 'I'm ready to go home. And I can't wait to have a shave!'

Chills shook his head. 'Wait and see. As soon as you get home, you'll be wanting to come back down.'

I wonder if I'll feel like that? Stay thought. The penguin chick sitting between her paws shook itself and gave a loud squawk.

'Here comes Dad!' Chills said.

The chick jumped off Stay's platform and started running down the rocks towards a shiny black-and-white adult that had just waddled out of the water. Other chicks nearby heard the sound and started chasing the adult too. Chills and Beakie laughed as the adult penguin turned and ran away, chased by about forty balls of fluff.

'We'd better start packing up,' Beakie said. 'They're sending the chopper for us tomorrow. The ship's due in a few days.'

Stay felt a moment of shock. She'd known they were going back, but hadn't realised how soon.

Chills walked over and picked her up. 'We'd better do a bit of fundraising back at the station, Stay. Can't have you going back to Australia half empty, eh?'

The fundraising! Stay hadn't collected any money since she arrived at Mawson and she'd forgotten all about her work while she'd been on Bechervaise Island. What if she had to go back to Hobart with almost nothing?

Suddenly all her memories of home came rushing back. Carol and Jet would still be wondering what had happened to her. The Guide Dog puppies would still be waiting for money for their training. She had responsibilities, and she felt bad at having forgotten them.

'Time for all of us to RTA,' Chills said as he turned for the hut.

What is RTA? Stay wondered.

'Return to Australia,' he said. 'Back to the real world.'

Chapter 34

The Squirrel helicopter hovered over the flat ledge of rock and then landed gently. Nuts was in the pilot seat, Stay saw, as he turned off the rotors and waved at them. His black beard had grown even longer.

Chills and Beakie had packed up all of their belongings and carried the bags far away from the penguins, right across to the other side of the island, so the birds wouldn't be disturbed by the sound of the helicopter. It had taken them many trips to get everything to a safe distance, and they were cold and tired.

Stay felt anxious. The penguin research had been finished successfully, but her own job in Antarctica wasn't over, and there wasn't much time left.

A cold wind was blowing, and the three men formed a chain and started passing the bags and boxes up to the helicopter.

'Hurry up!' Nuts called. 'If this wind picks up much more, I can't take off.'

Chills and Beakie started tossing the bundles to each other and Nuts quickly stowed them in the Squirrel's side cargo baskets.

'Hop in,' he called as they finished loading. 'And remember — Stay gets the front seat!'

'Are you kidding?' Beakie said. 'I want the front seat.'

Nuts shook his head. 'Sorry. She's my most famous passenger. Get in the back, chicken chasers.'

Chills lifted Stay into the front seat, buckled the harness around her, and put the headphones over her ears. He gave her a pat and a smile. 'You're a celebrity now, Stay,' he said, and climbed into the back seat.

Nuts started the helicopter and the rotors began spinning with a loud roar. They rose up in the air and Stay looked out eagerly to see the view. She loved flying.

The bay was filling up with flat pieces of ice that looked like giant pancakes. She could see Mawson Station ahead of them, its brightly coloured buildings standing out against the grey and brown rock. There had been a few snowfalls in the past week and snow was starting to pile up around the station.

Nuts pointed out in the direction of the sea as he turned the chopper. His voice crackled through the headphones. 'There's the ship!'

Stay, Chills and Beakie all looked where he was pointing. Stay could see a small orange shape in the distance making its way through the pancake ice. It was the *Aurora Australis*, coming to take them back to Hobart.

'There's been a change of plans, as usual, because of the ice conditions,' Nuts said. 'The ship went to Davis first to pick up passengers, so Mawson is her last stop. Should be arriving at the station by tomorrow. You haven't got much time to get organised. There's a farewell dinner tonight and then you're off home.'

Chills was silent, but Stay knew what he was thinking. If the ship had already been to Davis, then he wouldn't have a chance to say goodbye to Kaboom. And neither would Stay.

Stay looked back at Bechervaise Island one last time. As they rose higher in the air, she could see the two little apple huts that had been their home. She'd had lots of adventures in Antarctica, and being on Bechervaise, watching the penguins and seals and enjoying the company of Chills and Beakie, had been one of her favourites. Now it was time to go home.

But for some reason Stay didn't feel happy to see the *Aurora Australis* heading their way.

Chapter 35

To her surprise, Stay was the guest of honour at the Mawson Station farewell dinner. She had her own place setting at the head of one of the long tables. Chills put on her bow tie and tucked a white napkin into her harness, and the chef personally brought her a plate of beef stroganoff with rice and a glass of soft drink.

Of course she couldn't really drink or eat, but she liked the idea of it, and Chills, who was sitting by her side, was quite happy to eat her meal as well as his own.

She really had become famous over the summer and everyone wanted to pat her and take a photograph.

'No pats or pictures without a donation!' Chills said when people came up. 'It's good practice — in case you've forgotten how to use money.'

There was a bit of grumbling, as no one could remember where they'd put their cash, but after dinner people went back to quarters and found their hidden-away wallets. Stay posed for photographs with just about every single person on station, and coin after coin clanked down through her head, along with folded-up notes. By the time dinner was over, she was so heavy that Chills grunted when he picked her up.

Everyone went to the bar to celebrate the end of the summer season. Stay sat up on the bar and earnt even more donations when people came for a drink. Everyone patted her when they walked past and she enjoyed being the centre of attention.

'Sure you don't want to leave her down here?' Jackie asked. 'It doesn't seem fair to lose the huskies and Stay all at the same time.'

'I need to take her home,' Chills said. 'She belongs in Hobart. Sorry about that. The huskies will be good company for her on the ship.'

Stay felt her heart sink. She had forgotten that the huskies were going back to Hobart too. Of course they'd be on the *Aurora Australis* with her. Cocoa might be her friend now, but she knew that Blackie still hated her. It wouldn't be easy, sharing a ship with them.

'Bedtime,' Chills said, interrupting her thoughts. 'There'll be a big rush to get on the ship tomorrow and I've still got some packing to do. Come on, Stay. We're sleeping in one of the old dongas tonight. It'll be fun.'

He lifted her off the bar and carried her with both arms. Lots of hands reached out to pat her head as he walked through the crowd and Stay realised she would miss the expeditioners. They were unusual people, but very interesting. A big, strange, friendly family.

Chills and Stay stepped outside. It was dark and very cold. The sun had started setting again late in January and now the nights were almost a normal length, about nine hours. Stay had loved the long, lingering sunsets and sunrises, when the sky turned all different shades. She knew that by the end of May the sun would go down and not be seen again for six weeks.

Overhead Stay could see the Milky Way stretching across the sky. During summer she hadn't seen the stars much and she'd almost forgotten them. They looked very bright and close and, as they stood there, she saw a shooting star fall.

'Make a wish, Stay!' Chills said.

Before Stay could make her wish, a wave of green light suddenly swept across the sky, dimming the stars behind it. She'd never seen anything like it and she gazed in wonder.

'The southern lights!' Chills said. 'Isn't that beautiful? Lucky winterers get to see them all the time.'

Stay remembered the Boss telling her about the aurora australis and she was glad to have seen it herself. The two of them watched the green, glowing light in the sky, until finally Chills shivered. 'Come on, girl. Let's have that money out of you, and get packed up.'

Chills staggered along the road, skidding on the ice but managing to stay on his feet. He reached the line of old accommodation huts, where he had a bunk to sleep for his last night on station, and went inside.

It didn't take long for him to finish his packing and he turned Stay upside down to empty out the money into a sack and put it carefully in his bag. He took out one coin and slipped it back into her when he turned her up the right way.

'I'll get the Boss to put your money in the safe when we board the ship,' he said. 'I hope he's forgiven me for dognapping you, Stay.'

Stay hoped so too. She watched Chills get into bed, turn off the lamp and pull up the covers close to his chin. She could feel that he was sad.

'I wish I could have said goodbye to Kaboom,' he murmured. 'It would have been great to see Davis Station again too. I don't know when I'll get back down to Antarctica. I guess no one really knows. You only get your job for a year.' He rolled over and punched his pillow. 'Antarctica gets inside you, Stay. Once you've been down here, you always want to come back.'

He fell silent and a few minutes later Stay heard a quiet snore.

It was her last night on Antarctica. Although she'd been there for the whole summer, Stay felt like she'd only had a taste of Antarctic life. There were so many more places to explore and adventures to be had. She thought of Kaboom, who was staying down for winter and would get to see falling stars and the aurora australis nearly every day. She'd be there when the sea froze over and she could walk across the sea ice to the islands, or go exploring on the quad bikes or in a Hägg.

I'll miss you, Kaboom, Stay thought. Then she mentally shook herself. It was no good thinking about Kaboom. It was time for Stay to go back to Hobart and sit outside a supermarket again. It would be very dull compared to Antarctica, but on those long lonely nights she could relive all her Antarctic adventures. If she saw Jet again, she'd have so much to tell him.

Stay realised she'd forgotten to make a wish on the falling star. She didn't know what she wanted to wish for. *I'll save it up for when I really need it*, she thought.

Chapter 36

You again! Blackie snarled at Stay.

They were standing by the harbour, waiting for their turn on the barge that would take them out to the *Aurora Australis*, which was anchored just offshore. Windy and Baldy, with several other helpers, were holding on to the huskies to stop them fighting. Stay sat on top of Chills's bag, watching the barge push its way through the drifting ice towards the shore.

Stay sighed to herself. There was nothing she could do to make Blackie like her, so she decided to not even try.

Cocoa looked in her direction. *Hello, Stay. Haven't the puppies grown? They've been running with the sledge for the last two weeks. They're nearly ready to start working.*

Stay looked at the pups. Like the penguin chicks, they'd grown very fast and were catching up with the adult huskies. They had thick coats of fur and friendly brown eyes. It looked as though they took after their mother in temperament.

They look wonderful, she said to Cocoa.

But the dogs were all uneasy, Stay realised. She, at least, knew what to expect from their voyage. Now the dogs knew she'd been telling them the truth about leaving Antarctica, but they had no idea what the rest of the world was like. They were nervous and snappy.

It'll be fun, she thought to all of them. *You'll see trees and grass, and feel the rain. You can dig holes in the dirt. Everything smells amazing.*

None of the dogs knew what she was talking about, she realised. None of them had ever seen trees or grass, and it never rained in Antarctica. They'd find out for themselves soon enough, just as she had discovered snow and ice and blizzards.

The barge reached the loading dock and there was a rush of activity as everyone helped hand down the luggage. A crane lifted big baskets of cargo across to the barge, which sank lower and lower into the water.

'That's enough!' the barge skipper called. 'I'll be back soon for the next load. Get the dogs ready.'

As the barge pushed off, Stay heard the distant sound of the helicopter coming in to land. She wondered where Nuts had been. Perhaps helping to load cargo onto the ship.

There were plenty of other things to take her attention. The Boss and all the crew were over there on the ship. She wondered if the Boss had forgiven her for staying in Antarctica. She hoped he'd allow her on the Bridge again, and that he'd tell her more stories of sailing the world's oceans. She could watch out for whales and albatrosses from up there, and she'd be safe from Blackie. He wouldn't be allowed on the Bridge, Stay was pretty certain. The huskies were never allowed inside.

Stay heard footsteps running down the road towards the dock. From the corner of her eye she saw someone run up behind Chills and put big gloved hands over his eyes.

'Who's that?' Chills said.

'Me!'

It was Kaboom, Stay realised with a thrill.

'How did you get here?' Chills asked, turning around with a big grin on his face.

'Friends in high places,' Kaboom said. 'Nuts flew one of the Squirrels over for RTA. I got a lift with him. I had to come and say goodbye to Stay.'

'Oh, righteo,' Chills said, and his grin disappeared. 'There she is.'

Kaboom came over to Stay and crouched down beside her. She patted Stay on the head and then gave her a hug. She put her face up close.

'Do you really want to go home?' she whispered in Stay's ear. 'Or do you want to stay here in Antarctica?'

Chapter 37

Stay felt a pang of excitement. What did Kaboom mean? Was she about to be dognapped?

Kaboom gave her another hug and whispered again. 'If you want to stay, let me know. And then keep very, very quiet, no matter what happens.'

She stood up again and patted Stay on the head. 'You're the most famous Antarctic dog of all now,' she said loudly. 'We'll miss you.' She turned back to Chills and Beakie. 'How was your time on Beche?'

Stay was too churned up to listen to their replies. Like Chills, she had to go back to the real world. She had responsibilities, and a job to do. She belonged to the Royal Guide Dogs and she should be sitting outside the supermarket where Carol had put her, collecting money.

She remembered all the months she had spent outside shops in Hobart as a collection dog. It had been cold and lonely. Nothing much changed around her and she didn't move from place to place. Adults mostly ignored her, though children usually stopped to say hello and give her a pat. It was a noble life, but not very exciting.

If she stayed in Antarctica, Chills would go back without her. She might never see him again! *But if I go back to being a collection dog, I won't be with Chills anyway,* she thought. *I'll be alone, out on the streets.*

Stay felt like her head was spinning. She loved Chills and wanted to stay with him. She was loyal to the Guide Dogs and wanted to do her job well. And she loved Antarctica too!

She loved it even more than Chills and the Royal Guide Dogs, she realised. It was big and frightening and wild, but every day in Antarctica was an adventure. The people were like no other people she'd ever met, and there were amazing animals like penguins and seals and skuas and snow petrels.

If she stayed with Kaboom, she'd become a winterer. She'd see the aurora in the sky. She'd see the sun set and not rise for six weeks. She'd see snow and ice and icebergs and go on jollies across the sea ice to new places.

She'd be the only dog in Antarctica.

Stay looked over at the huskies. The barge was on its way back and they knew they were being loaded onto it.

They looked miserable. They didn't want to leave. They were scared of what might be ahead.

Stay had an idea. It was time to use her wish, the one she'd saved from the falling star.

Chapter 38

Stay sent her wish out as hard as she could: *I WANT TO STAY.*

Kaboom took a step closer to Chills. 'Actually, I also came to say goodbye to you. I'll miss you.'

A little smile spread over Chills's face. 'I'll miss you too. Hope I can see you when you get back.'

'That'd be cool,' Kaboom said. She put her arms around him and gave him a big hug. They held on to each other for so long that people started cheering.

Suddenly Stay felt a hand on her back. Nuts was crouching behind the boxes with a big mailbag. While everyone was clapping and watching Kaboom and Chills, Nuts grabbed Stay and slid her into the bag so fast that nobody saw.

As he started carrying the bag away, Stay heard a growl. No human had seen Nuts take her, but Blackie, with his sharp eyes, had noticed the dognapping. If he started barking now, she'd be found and she'd have to go back on the ship.

Blackie? She sent a thought towards him. *If you get scared on the ship —*

I'm not scared! he growled.

Of course not. What I meant was — if Chills gets scared, can you keep him company?

Blackie paused. Stay could tell that Nuts was making good progress carrying her. She only needed another minute or two and he'd be away from the dock and able to hide her somewhere.

Blackie, Chills is really sad about leaving. He needs a friend. He needs you.

It was true, and Stay felt a pain in her chest. It was so hard to leave Chills that she nearly couldn't do it. But Chills and Blackie could be friends. They could look after each other.

Blackie gave a little whine. *All right. I'll look after him.*

Stay heard the sound of a door opening. She was being carried inside a building. Nuts seemed to be climbing and then she felt herself being shoved into a small space.

Nuts gave a giggle. 'They'll never find you here, Stay. Don't worry, we'll be back real soon. Just as soon as the ship casts off.'

197

Chapter 39

Stay looked down through the window of the Twin Otter. She was strapped into the front seat and wearing headphones. Beside her, Nuts was piloting. Kaboom was in the back.

Below on the ocean, the *Aurora Australis* was steaming away from the station, smoke rising from its stack.

Chills had started searching for Stay when he realised she was missing, and it was the hardest thing Stay had ever done to stay quiet when she heard him calling her name. *You won't be with Chills anyway,* she'd kept telling herself, *not once you get back to Hobart.*

He hadn't called her for long. The ship was ready to leave and it wouldn't wait for anything. Chills and the huskies had gone across on the final barge trip and been loaded, along with the last of the cargo.

Nuts and Kaboom had rescued Stay from her hiding place in the roof cavity of the old aircraft hangar near the loading area. They smuggled her to the Hägg before anyone from Mawson could find her, and set off for the summer airstrip. The Squirrels were both going back on the ship, so they were using the Twin Otter to return to Davis.

After the little plane had taken off, Nuts made a low sweep over the station so that the Mawson winterers could see Stay in the front seat. They all waved and cheered.

'Well, the Mawsonites are pretty happy that you're staying,' Nuts said. He lifted the Twin Otter in the air and turned it in the direction of the ship. 'Think Chills will ever forgive you?' he asked Kaboom.

'I don't know,' Kaboom said. 'It was a mean trick.'

Stay could hear Kaboom's unspoken thoughts above the hissing in the headphones. *It wasn't just a trick. I really did want to say goodbye to him.*

I know, Stay thought back.

I know you do, Kaboom thought.

Stay could hear her thoughts even more clearly than she could hear Chills's. Kaboom was going to be a great friend.

'OK, we're heading down,' Nuts said. Stay remembered how much she loved flying as Nuts put the plane into a close turn around the ship.

They were at eye level with the Bridge and Stay could see everyone was gathered there for their departure.

Someone pointed at the plane and everyone turned. Nuts gave a cheeky wave at the Boss.

The radio crackled and the Boss's voice came into the headphones. 'I see you have a fugitive on board, Nuts.'

'That's right, Captain,' Nuts said. 'Stay didn't want to RTA.'

'Lucky the money she's raised *is* going to RTA,' the Boss said. 'Otherwise you'd be in big trouble.'

They were almost past the Bridge and Stay couldn't see Chills among the faces looking out the window. What had happened to him?

'There he is,' Kaboom said, pointing.

Chills was standing on the helideck at the back of the ship, holding Blackie. As the plane circled, he looked up. Stay felt that pain in her chest again when she saw the expression on his face.

'Oh, Chills, I'm sorry,' Kaboom said, though there was no way Chills could hear her.

I'm sorry, Stay thought. *I'll miss you. We both will.*

'I feel so mean,' Kaboom said. 'Let's get out of here.'

Nuts turned the plane and as they passed the ship for the final time, Stay saw Chills give a little smile and a wave.

You belong in Antarctica, Stay, she heard him think. *Bye.*

Blackie barked in their direction and then pressed closer to Chills as the plane started heading inland, back in the direction of Davis.

They'll be all right, Stay thought to Kaboom as the ship disappeared behind them. She thought that her friend might have had a little tear on her cheek. Stay would have had her own tears too, if she could cry.

'Have you given Stay her passport yet?' Nuts asked.

'Oh, no, I forgot!' Kaboom said, and wiped her eyes. 'Here, Stay. Now that you're an official Antarctican, you need a passport. With a stamp for everywhere that you visit. I've put the Mawson Station stamp in it already.'

She reached over the seat and fastened a small blue book on a chain to Stay's leg.

'Now everyone will know what adventures you've been on,' she said. 'You've only just begun exploring Antarctica. You'll see incredible stars and the southern lights. You'll get snotsicles when it's really cold and your snot freezes. We'll go out to the field huts and the Prince Charles Mountains. You might go on a traverse to Law Dome — that's a long way away on the plateau. In spring we'll visit the Chinese Station and drop by to see the Russians. You might even get to McMurdo one day. Everyone wants to meet the last dog in Antarctica.'

Stay felt herself smiling. Not a smile that anyone could see, but a great big smile right inside her, a smile that didn't go away as the Twin Otter flew over the snow and ice and she saw mountains and glaciers rising up in front of them.

She was a real Antarctican now. She was staying.

After you've read this book ...

Stay was dognapped from Hobart in 1991. Her arrival in Antarctica coincided with the end of Australia's use of huskies, a tradition that began with Sir Douglas Mawson on his voyage in 1911 and was carried on when Mawson Station was established in 1954. The last two teams of huskies in Antarctica, including Blackie, Cocoa and the puppies Misty, Cobber and Frosty, returned to Hobart in 1992 as part of changes due to the Madrid Protocol for the environmental protection of Antarctica. The older dogs retired and lived out their days in Tasmania. The younger dogs and the puppies made an epic journey of their own, ending up in Ely, Minnesota, near the Canadian border, where they continued working. The story of their departure from Antarctica was made into a film, *The Last Husky* (Aurora Films). Misty's ashes were taken back to Antarctica in 2011.

When Stay first met the huskies of Mawson, they showed their disgust at being replaced by weeing on her, an incident captured in at least one photograph.

After the end of her first season in Antarctica, Stay didn't want to 'RTA'. It seems she had a mind of her own, for instead of returning to the Royal Guide Dogs full of money, she stayed in Antarctica and began a life of grand adventure and subterfuge as the last dog on the continent.

Since then, Stay has been smuggled, hidden, freed and dognapped so many times that she's lost count. She has travelled around Antarctica on helicopters, aeroplanes, skidoos, Häggs, quad bikes, tractors and utes. She's hidden everywhere from mailbags to cargo holds to roof spaces. She has been a wintering expeditioner at every Australian base and Macquarie Island, and has visited the Antarctic bases and ships of many other countries.

Stay lost her leg in an accident at Mawson in 1993 and it was replaced by a carpenter known as 'Smoothie'. Her lost leg was sent back to Davis Station with a note saying, *This is all you're getting.*

After many other adventures, and long periods where no one knew her location, in 2002 Stay was kidnapped from Mawson and travelled to the other end of the globe, ending up in the Ny Ålesund international research station in Spitsbergen, the world's most northerly settlement, where she was photographed in front of the Roald Amundsen memorial. She made it back to Davis Station in time for the next season.

Stay's original passport fell apart and was lost, but she has a more recent one that's also full of stamps. She makes regular appearances in the newsletters and reports of each station and her antics are closely followed. She even has her own Facebook page, though her updates are erratic and mysterious.

Over the years Royal Guide Dogs Tasmania asked for Stay's return a few times, but eventually realised she was never coming back. There have been several collections and donations from Antarctic expeditioners to the association over the years.

If you see one of Stay's relatives sitting patiently in a shopping centre or airport, please give her a coin to help with the training of a Guide Dog. Stay will be very grateful.

Antarctica and global warming

'Global warming' is the increase in temperatures scientists have been observing around the world over the past few decades. These increases are believed to be caused by the amount of greenhouse gases, such as carbon dioxide, methane and nitrous oxide, that humans are releasing into the atmosphere.

While scientists have known for a while that the Antarctic Peninsula is warming rapidly, they thought temperatures in other parts of the continent were fairly stable. However, research announced in late 2012 showed that West Antarctica is warming nearly twice as fast as scientists previously believed. Between 1958 and 2010, temperatures in West Antarctica increased by 2.4 degrees Celsius. That makes it one of the fastest-warming places on the planet.

While global warming will be serious for all humans and other creatures, it may have very dramatic effects in Antarctica. The West Antarctic ice sheet is up to four kilometres thick, and if it melts or even partly melts because of global warming, it will make a big contribution to rising sea levels.

Living creatures in Antarctica — especially on the Antarctic Peninsula — are already feeling the effects of climate change. According to the British Antarctic Survey, the numbers of Adélie penguins, which need sea ice, are dropping, while other species such as chinstrap penguins, which like open water, are increasing and plants are starting to grow on parts of the peninsula.

The research projects and weather observations carried out by nations that have Antarctic bases — including Australia — are making an important contribution to our understanding of climate change.

Thank you

I met Stay during my six-week voyage to Antarctica in late 2011. As a 'round tripper', I only had a brief taste of life on an Antarctic station, and had to rely on the help of others to make sure this tale was as realistic as a story about a telepathic fibreglass dog could be. Any mistakes are mine, not theirs.

Thank you to my team of Antarctic readers and fact checkers from the 2011/12 Antarctic season, including Graham 'Cookie' Cook ('outgoing' Davis Station leader — a genial person, plus he was heading back to Hobart), Bob Heath (an Antarctic pilot who was tragically killed in a Twin Otter crash in Antarctica in 2013), Stephanie MacDonald (weather observer and brave twice-daily releaser of the hydrogen-filled balloon), Timo Viehl (clever German atmospheric scientist who worried about his English grammar, though it was better than most native speakers') and Louise Carroll (weather forecaster who hurt her hand slipping over on ice on her second day in Antarctica and was nearly sent straight back home).

Dave 'Fluffy' Hosken (scientist of complicated things related to lasers and champion beard-grower) helped with reading and fact checking, but I am mostly grateful to him for taking me on an unforgettable three-day field trip to Bandits Hut and Platcha Hut, and allowing me to use some of his photographs. He dognapped Stay from the Davis LQ so she could come with us in the Hägglunds, foiling the plans of Mawson expeditioners who'd planned to steal her and take her to Bechervaise Island, and unwittingly sparking the idea for this story.

Thanks to Margie Law, Jane Wasley and Mali Greenlaw for reading the manuscript and also putting me up in their house in Hobart, which I'm sure felt like the Antarctic halfway hotel by the end of the season. Thanks to Erica Adamson, expeditioner, who spent four summers and one winter in Antarctica in the late 1980s and early 1990s, for her comments.

Julie McInness came down on the same voyage as me to study penguins on Bechervaise Island over summer. Her emails home, consisting of fantastic penguin photos with clever captions, made me laugh out loud and she kindly answered my numerous questions about penguins and life on Bechervaise.

Hazel Edwards, another red-headed writer who has been to Antarctica on an arts fellowship, also wrote some children's stories about Stay that she kindly shared with me.

Antarctic station leader Jeremy Smith wrote 'A short biography of Stay' in 2003, which was helpful in piecing together her travels, and journalist Jo Chandler's article 'Plastic pooch still guarding Antarctic sub-cult', which appeared in *The Age* on 18 January 2010, gave a humorous take on why Stay has gathered a cult following, suggesting that she has become a talisman of the proud culture of independence and wackiness that lives on in Antarctica today.

The Australian Antarctic Division (AAD) has run an arts fellowship program since the early 1980s, sending artists of all kinds, including writers, filmmakers, photographers, artists, musicians and dancers, to visit Antarctica. Thanks to the AAD for awarding me the 2011/12 Antarctic Arts Fellowship, so I could sail for six weeks on the *Aurora Australis* and visit Antarctica. AAD marketing and events manager Kristin Raw cheerfully encouraged me to apply for three years running and was most helpful before and after my voyage.

Voyage leader Sharon Labudda and deputy leader Leanne Millhouse made the trip a pleasure, along with Captain Murray Doyle, who has been the master of

RSV *Aurora Australis* since 1995 (he is not 'the Boss' of this story) and the always-friendly ship's crew, whose fundraising efforts for Camp Quality over the years have seen thousands of dollars raised for that charity.

Thanks to my companions, the expeditioners heading down to Antarctica for the 2011/12 summer, and those hardy souls who had spent the previous winter there and returned on the ship with me.

Diana Patterson, Australia's first female station leader in Antarctica, wrote a wonderful book about her experiences called *The Ice Beneath My Feet*. Diana was station leader at Mawson in 1989 and went on several sledging trips with Mawson's famous huskies before they were returned to Australia. Thanks, Diana, for helping me understand station life in that era.

Thanks to my agent, Sophie Hamley, and all at publisher HarperCollins, particularly Cristina Cappelluto, Lisa Berryman and Kate O'Donnell.

My niece Aimee Blackadder read the first few chapters of this book when I started writing and made me promise to finish it. Her obsession with reading is a delight and inspiration.

And thanks to my partner, Andi Davey, who hates the cold but would really love to meet Stay one day.

Jesse Blackadder wanted to be a vet from the age of five, but ended up becoming a writer. She lives near an extinct volcano in northern New South Wales, and shares her very big garden with a water dragon called Kinky, a koala called Blinky, a python called Slinky and lots of other wild creatures. She was lucky enough to meet the real Stay when she went to Antarctica on an arts fellowship, and was involved in a dognapping incident at Davis Station.

Jesse Blackadder

PARAKU

The Desert Brumby

Jesse Blackadder

RINGO

The Lost Flying Fox